*Praise for*

# THE GODDESS TWINS

"*The Goddess Twins* is a fantastic ride, viewed through the eyes of girls on the verge of adulthood . . . Twins Arden and Aurora are at once teenagers tackling contemporary issues and immortals in training, learning to harness their supernatural gifts in the face of adversity. I thoroughly enjoyed this novel, and can't wait for it to reach its readers!"
— DEVI S. LASKAR, award-winning author of
*The Atlas of Reds and Blues*

"If you are ready to claim the superpowers you know have always been within you, Arden and Aurora—*The Goddess Twins*—are here to light your way! . . . Don't be scared if you experience some flashes of *The Matrix* subway scene; spaces in *Sense8*; channel a bit of Octavia Butler as well as Zadie Smith—maybe even *Riot Baby*, too."
— VALERIE HAYNES PERRY, author and motivational
writing coach of valeriehaynesperry.com and
motivationalwriting.com

"*The Goddess Twins* is an addictive YA novel that will live on in the minds of readers long after the final page. Williams weaves characters so real they leap out of the story and into your imagination . . . A spellbinding tale rich with enchantment and lore. Girl-power meets modern magic. Unforgettable."
— ALEXIS MARIE CHUTE, award-winning author of
The 8th Island Trilogy

# THE
# GODDESS
# TWINS

# THE
# GODDESS
# TWINS

*A Novel*

## YODASSA WILLIAMS

Published by SparkPress, a BookSparks imprint,
A division of SparkPoint Studio, LLC
Phoenix, Arizona, USA, 85007
www.gosparkpress.com

Published 2020
Printed in the United States of America
ISBN: 978-1-68463-032-5 (pbk)
ISBN: 978-1-68463-033-2 (e-bk)

Library of Congress Control Number: 2019954595

*Book design by Stacey Aaronson*

As a child, I knew that writers are magicians.
I quietly craved but feared to believe that I—small, brown,
awkward me—could harness the power to weave worlds
and stir emotions from markings on a page.
This novel is dedicated to her, my inner child, who knew
this story needed to exist and always dreamed she would
become an alchemist of words.

Also: for Channelle.

*A*s Ezekiel paces the length of the bare room, the eyes of his son and grandson remain fixed on him. He had barely aged over the centuries of his eternal life, but Ezekiel's muscular frame and handsome features grew colder each year, sharpened by his dark thoughts for vengeance against The Fates and his goddess wife, Ghani. After wiping a band of sweat from his dusky brown forehead, he continues to tread the wooden floor of their rented farmhouse. It is nearly midnight on a balmy summer evening in Kingston, Jamaica; the year is 2020. In this year, Ezekiel's granddaughters will turn eighteen. And Ezekiel's seemingly endless decades of plotting will turn into action.

As his long legs command the space like a panther in a cage, Ezekiel huffs dismissively at his weak son, Teresh. Also blessed with eternal life, Teresh resembles a young man in his thirties—but his slight physique and propensity for shortness of breath exasperates Ezekiel, reminding him all too much of past failures. Ezekiel smiles with pride as he passes the brawny form of his grandson, who has lived over a hundred human years but appears a decade younger than Teresh. His grandson is the key to his revenge, the solution to Ezekiel's quest for power. The time has finally come to move him into position.

That very morning, after their usual silent breakfast of cornmeal porridge and freshly picked fruit, Ezekiel told the two men he had an announcement to deliver after dinner. Ezekiel then spent most of the day in town, arranging for their international travel and lodging. Arranging for the abduction. Everything was going according to the plan he had begun to hatch exactly one hundred years ago. After hours of farm chores, physical training, and recitations of Ezekiel's manifesto, the three men ate their typical end-of-day meal with heads lowered, and then gathered in the small living room of the farmhouse. As Ezekiel stands before his son and grandson now, still wearing one of his best suits from a busy day of taking action, he feels a moment of pride that he's dressed so appropriately to deliver this historic announcement.

"It is our duty to reclaim the world the goddesses have allowed destroyed, is it not?" He pauses and faces his kin, waiting for affirmation of their shared mission.

"Yes, it is," they reply, nodding in unison. Ezekiel gazes past them, then plows forward as if they had not spoken.

"Since Ghani and her daughters received their powers two centuries ago, all we have seen is the destruction of our world and the subjugation of our people of color! Our men, our black kings, have no power in this world. The goddesses have squandered their power, using it for vanity in the face of the suffering. It is up to us to make things right, is it not?" Ezekiel's voice booms, echoing on the tin roof.

"Yes, it is!" the men reply, louder than the first time,

with more urgency. Ezekiel continues his pacing, then stops abruptly.

"For so long," he hisses, "for an entire century, all we had was a plan. An idea of how to set the balance right. We have had to hide and lay in wait for the perfect time to seize the power we need to reshape the world in our image. Grandson—I have formed you into the perfect weapon and warrior against the goddesses. The time for action is upon us. Are you ready?"

"Of course, Grandfather. You can trust that I am more than ready," his grandson replies, standing taller in reaction to the announcement. Ezekiel had told him that since before his birth, he had been primed for a special purpose. Over the last century, one of Ezekiel's main focuses was to show his grandson how the world really worked. How white supremacy controlled wealth, justice, health, opportunity, and every other aspect of society. How the constant corruption and suppression of the black man stemmed from racism, hatred, and fear. And how all the goddesses just stood by, hoarding their powers, doing nothing as the world fell apart.

Ezekiel places his hand on his grandson's shoulder and squeezes the hardened muscle. He could not be any more proud; his grandson had been a perfect student in every way. Out of the corner of his eye, Ezekiel catches Teresh tighten his jaw and swallow thickly. He can practically feel the bitterness radiating off of him and knows he is frustrated over his insignificant role in the master plan. But this is no time to address his son's resentment. And Ezekiel knows that Teresh will remain loyal; he has nowhere else to go.

Clearing his throat, Ezekiel resumes his heavy steps across the hardwood floor. He watches a pair of mosquitos fly in front of the light before speaking. "I have set into motion the events that will lead you to your ascension, Grandson," Ezekiel proclaims. "Tonight we leave Jamaica to begin preparations in London. The power that is to be yours is ripe for taking. The twins will be eighteen in less than a week. Once you gain their powers of telepathy and telekinesis, there will be nothing and no one that can stop us from setting the Earth the way it should be." Ezekiel feels his face slowly break into a smile as he considers the day's events.

"Today I made a phone call that will pull Selene away from her daughters. We will capture her, and once the twins rush to her aid, you, my grandson, will have the opportunity to take from them the powers they falsely inherited."

"But Father, wouldn't it be easier to just kidnap the girls from wherever they are now?" Teresh interjects.

Ezekiel stops his pacing, turns, and lays a heavy slap to his only son's face. "Only an ignorant mind would suggest an option that does not take into account all the necessary variables," Ezekiel rebukes. Teresh stays silent, visibly working out his jaw from his father's hit. As Ezekiel looks away in disgust, he spies the pair of mosquitoes now caught in a spider's web in the darkened upper corner of the room. He smiles darkly and turns to the two men.

"Listen well. Neither Selene's nor her daughters' talents or will to survive should be underestimated. We must be like the cunning arachnid, crafting a trap, preying on their weaknesses to pull the enemy into our hands." Ezekiel weaves his fingers together, locking his palms tightly, glancing at the mosquitoes again. "The twins were born in London on October 12. So it is there, at midnight, on their eighteenth birthday that you, my grandson, will have the chance to break the veil around their inheritance, to take advantage of the window of opportunity, and absorb their powers."

Ezekiel stands squarely in front of his grandson, the same rage fueling him radiating toward his kin. "Their power *belongs* to you. You are the first and only power conduit of our family. You are the beacon of truth that the men, gods, should rule over—not only this family, but the world. This is your birthright. I have done all I can to ensure your success in defeating the twins and taking your place as god and conqueror of all."

Ezekiel and his grandson nod at one another. Sacrifice and cunning had gotten them this far, and Ezekiel knew much more would be necessary to take them to glory.

"We leave for London tonight," Ezekiel continues. "I've found a warehouse for us. Once we land, we will begin fueling you up to your highest capacity. We'll find a hundred girls for you to absorb, if that's what it takes! You must be your strongest and fastest to take their powers. In the end, the twins will be dead, yes—but what can we do if it is for the greater good?" Ezekiel shrugs, then smiles broadly. "We will finally give white supremacy something to fear that cannot be defeated. Are you ready for your destiny, grandson?"

"Yes. I am ready."

# I

## Arden
# THE HARD WAY

*T*he biggest frustration of my life? Having someone who looks exactly like me running around doing things I would never ever do myself. Though I've not been invited, this house party is inescapable. Even my noise cancelling headphones are useless against the thumping bass pounding the walls like the big bad wolf trying to get into a piglet's house. Glass shatters loudly, and I think, *Great, that sounded like something expensive.* The sound is followed by an eruption of people shouting, "Yeah! Turn it up!" and applauding as the music volume is hiked even higher. The bass pounds harder: *Thump. Thump. Thumpidy.*

I close my eyes and imagine myself transported somewhere else—somewhere calm, quiet, another universe where I'm flying through the clouds with a flock of technicolored birds, or exploring a planet full of humming mountains. Or even a universe like this one, but where I'm an only child, able to finish writing my new fantasy story in peace, far away from the fevered party happening inside my home. I open my eyes as I hear a girl screech loudly in delight, probably at something stupid, like a keg stand contest. I hear the screech again and realize it's my twin sister. I wonder what sound she'd make if I strangled her? Not that I ever would. It's just a thought—a fleeting but frequent one.

"Wow, you two are identical twins. That must be so exciting, right?"

Rule number one of identical twinning: Strangers love to say this to you. In amazement they take in our matching dimpled cheeks, dark toffee skin, and wide brown eyes. I am an expert in blocking the urge to roll my eyes.

Rule number two of identical twinning? Having a twin is so not the incredible delight people assume it to be. Just because we look alike doesn't mean we think alike.

People love pointing out our similarities, but if you take a real look, it's totally easy to tell us apart. Aurora prefers her hair bone straight, while I leave my thick curls natural, like a halo around my face. She's obsessed with fashion, mixing high and low with her own original designs. I'm more likely to be found at the library than the mall, wearing cardigans, tees, and skirts on the regular. Aurora calls it my "vintage schoolgirl thing," usually in a loving, inside-joke kind of way. I say "usually" because when my sister goes all mean girl, she can turn anything into a dagger. Just this morning she looked at my outfit and asked if I was on my way to desegregate a school. I gave her the middle finger. But she'd turned her back to me, so I didn't achieve the ideal effect.

Ugh! I've been staring at the same unfinished sentence for nearly half an hour! I close my laptop and place my headphones on my desk in defeat. Was it really just a month ago that my sister and I were laughing together at the movies and talking about the colleges we're applying to together? Sometimes I look at Aurora and feel so ridiculously lucky to be an identical twin. No one could ever understand me better than she does—like, all she has to do is look at my face and she knows where I'm at completely. There's a kind of magic that flows between us sometimes that I can't imagine surviving without. But other times? Other times I wish I could just crawl inside her mind and laser away the bits of her personality that make her the most irritating person I've ever known. Like this afternoon, when Aurora announced she'd posted online that she was throwing a massive house party.

"What? No!" I shook my head frantically. "Just because we have the house alone, doesn't mean you should invite everyone you know over tonight!"

"Well, I know you, and you're not invited. So there's that," she said with a smirk. "Plus, it's only a good party if people you don't know show up. I'm expecting this to be legendary."

There was no talking her out of it. Barely an hour later, the horde started to arrive. Thanks to the speed of teen word of mouth, hundreds of kids have congregated, intent on making the night "legendary," trashing our home from front to back in the process. It feels like an earthquake is hitting a zoo downstairs. Earlier, I watched the back lawn get trashed during a spontaneous group mudwrestling contest where absolutely no one was the winner. Then someone set off fireworks in the front yard, catching the bushes on fire. Thankfully someone was sober enough to grab the extinguisher and put it out. It's clear that Aurora has purposefully summoned madness to our door and I can do nothing to stop it.

I keep waiting for the cops to arrive or for someone to need to go to the ER. Something supremely bad is going to happen tonight. I just know it. My body aches and I feel sick to my stomach. It's been brewing all day, since the moment Mom left. Now I feel like I'm watching someone conjure the apocalypse. Aurora is pulling us both into a place from which we may never return. All because she's hurt and mad at our Mom.

So, LET ME back up and give you the tea on our Mom, Selene Bryant. Rated by multiple magazines as one of the most beautiful women alive, our mother is a recently retired and sickeningly famous opera singer. Despite her supposed retirement, she left Ohio, and us, this afternoon to be an emergency replacement for the lead in *Aida* in London.

So, that probably doesn't sound like too big of a deal, and it wouldn't be, if it weren't for two major things. One, in three days, it's our eighteenth birthday, and Mom's going to miss it for a performance. And two, by going back to work, Mom's breaking a promise she made to me and Aurora. An important one.

Mom went into retirement two years ago because Aurora had begged her to let us all stay in one place, together, like a normal family for once in our lives. Mom promised we could. She swore that she was done with the shows and the travelling, that there would be no more performances while we were finishing high school here in Cincinnati. But this morning before school, we woke up to her cooking breakfast. This was the first sign that something was off, because our mom never cooks. Over burned toast and runny eggs, she coughed nervously and said, "So, I may be gone before you get back from school for . . . a thing. And this thing might mean I'm away for a few days. And I want to be back before your birthday on Sunday, but I think I won't be. But everything is fine—more than fine—okay, girls?"

"What?" Aurora said, dropping her fork loudly onto her plate. "If you say it's for a performance, I swear I'm going to lose it."

"No, honey. Well, actually, yes. I'm afraid it is, for *Aida*. They need me to fill in in London for a few days. See, Diana Guarardi, you remember her, right? The wonderful soprano? She was at your christening! Well, she's come down with some type of swine bird flu or something, and wouldn't you know, the understudy and two other performers have the same thing, and they're just beside themselves trying to figure out how the show can go on, and they begged, darling, they literally begged, and can I say I do owe James, who is directing, like, three dozen favors, and of course he has called them in for this. He was absolutely begging. What was I to do?"

"Not say yes," Aurora whispered through grit teeth.

"Well . . . I just had to. I had to say yes. I'll be leaving this afternoon. Leo will come look in on you in the morning, but I'll be gone before you're back from school, I'm afraid." Mom's eyes darted to the dining room floor, and when I followed the look, I saw her bags, already packed. Aurora stared at the suitcases for a full minute, then got up from the table without a word. Mom looked so sad as her eyes followed Aurora up the stairs.

So, the timing of this international gig is horrible, yes. But the only real option available was to be happy Mom was given a chance to return to her life's passion. Our mother may be flighty in her relationships and passionate about her career, but just because she embraces opportunity, that doesn't mean she hates her children.

"You're doing a really excellent thing, saving the show. It must go on, and I'm sure it's going to be great." I held Mom's hand from across the table. "And we'll be okay on our own. Don't worry."

She nodded but looked back upstairs with a heavy sigh.

Before I left for school, I made sure to hug her long and tight, so much so that her mermaid pendant left a dent in my cheek. Aurora, on the other hand, kept her arms crossed against a hug. Her headphones on, she just stared at the bags on the floor then left the house in a huff.

"Please ignore the fact that one of your daughters has the emotional intelligence of a two-year-old," I said to Mom as we watched Aurora head out.

Mom chuckled and cradled my face in her hands, stroking my cheek with her thumb. "Can you promise me to look after your sister? To stay together while I'm gone, please?"

"Of course," I said way too quickly. Because it's actually nearly impossible to look after Aurora when she's determined to be a nightmare.

I thought about my family all day. When we returned from school, I confronted Aurora about her pissy attitude. Someone had to tell her about herself, and as usual, that someone would be me. When I knocked on her bedroom door, I was semi-confident I could get Aurora to see Mom's side of things. But when my sister finally appeared, she rolled her eyes heavily at me with her phone plastered to her ear.

"Do you mind?" she hissed and turned away. "Oh, it's no one, just my annoying twin," she said into the phone.

Ouch, I am *no one*? *Just* an annoying twin?

"Aurora, can we talk, please?" I asked, my frustration simmering. "This is important." She continued talking on her phone, so I tried again. "Leo won't be checking in on us till the morning. Mom is gone, and I know you're upset. Can we just talk about what's going on?" She ignored me. Again. But I plowed forward. "You barely said goodbye to Mom this morning. How could you be so rude to her? You know she loves us more than anything."

Aurora snorted and finally walked towards me. "You are such a tragedy," she said, pulling the phone away with a smirk. "News flash, Ar," she continued, her neck snapping with attitude as she stood me down. "Mom couldn't care less about the fact that she has *again* abandoned us for her need for attention. And you make me sick just feeding into her whole diva persona, like it's okay for her to up and leave, like she has no responsibility to be with her children days before their most important birthday yet? It's so easy for her to ditch us, like we're annoying accessories to her life. Now get out of my room. And do me the huge favor of staying away from me for the next four days."

"So, you've decided to be horrible to me, too? What did I do to you?" I demand.

"Steal my face!" she yells. "I'm sick of you spreading your patheticness all over these parts. Look, I'm throwing a party tonight, and I just can't have you embarrassing me, so consider yourself officially not invited."

She slammed the door on my foot, but not before howling, "Ruby Bridges," at my khaki skirted overalls and light pink Peter Pan-collared shirt. But as far as I'm concerned, no insult was made. "Sticks and stones," I muttered, limping away.

So, TO BE clear, I'm not upset about the disinvite thing. And I'm not begrudging people who like parties—just people who launch all-night ragers out of spite, like my sister. Doesn't she know that teen house parties *never ever* end well? Why does she *always* feel the need to learn a lesson the hard way?

Some partier jiggles the handle of my door, startling me. I breathe a sigh of relief when they find it locked, but when I hear knocking, my heart jumps.

"Hey. Hey, you in there?" a deep voice asks. I freeze, hoping he'll go away, but the knocking continues. "Hello? Bueller?"

I slide away from my desk and slowly approach the door. "What do you want?" I yell through the wood.

"You *are* in there!" the voice responds, excited.

Who *is* this person? "Yeah, it's my house and my room."

"Right, okay. So, I'm not sure if you know this, but there's a giant ass party going on in your house right now. Like, right downstairs even. You should come out."

"I'm aware," I yell back. "But I wasn't invited."

"Woah, that's shady. Or is this, like, some reverse VIP room type shit?"

"What? No." I shake my head with a chuckle. Okay, so he's a comedian, huh?

"You sure about that? Does the reverse VIP room come with champagne? Or is it only overflowing with shame?"

"Wow, ouch!" I giggle. "Thanks for that. You can go now."

"Wait, where's the bathroom up here?"

"The guest bathroom is downstairs."

"Yes, but see, the beautiful party host is currently destroying it with more puke than I've ever seen in my life."

I cringe. Great, Aurora's a wasted mess-opotamia. Just like a few years ago in Prague when she nearly drank herself into a coma after arguing with Mom that she was done living like a wealthy vagabond. "I should go help my sister," I say, to both myself and the voice. I open my door.

On the other side, I find a tall and well-built, deep brown skinned guy, so magnetically good looking I feel dizzy taking him in. A fitted black tee stretches across his broad chest. A goatee perfectly frames his mouth. His short dreads are tight, neat, and very sexy. But it's when his eyes lock with mine for the first time something weird happens. Everything dims around me. My sight is consumed by a vision of this guy and me locked together, kissing passionately in the back row of a nearly empty theater. In the scene, he pauses a moment, pulls away from me. He holds my face and kisses my cheeks, whispering, "I love you so much, Arden." I answer, "I love you too, Devin."

I shake my head and snap back to the present. My heart thumps loudly. I bite my lip and step backward into my room, looking away from the man standing in front of me.

*What the absolute hell was that?* It's like I stepped into one of those VR games Aurora loves, the kind that suck you out of your world and place you in another. But I'm not wearing a headset. *Was I transported somewhere? Watching a memory I've never lived? Where did that vision come from?*

"Do you mind if I come in?" the stranger asks, stepping into my room. "Your spot is awesome. Nice poster," he says, nodding at my Florence and the Machine concert banner. "She's unreal live."

"Yeah, she's a family friend," I mumble to the mermaids woven into my teal colored rug, my breathing returning to normal.

Okay, it may sound babyish, a mermaid carpet, but there's something about mermaids that has always calmed me. Mom is obsessed with them, too.

"Oh, so my name is Devin by the way," the stranger says over his shoulder.

My head whips up and I watch him as he inspect the walls of my room. I blink several times, struggling to process his presence. It's so intense, I can feel the body heat emanating from him affecting me from all the way over there. *Okay, there's a young man in my room.* My eyes drink in his body, noting that his jeans fit very, very well. I bite my lip, catching myself. *Hormones, please chill. I need to think, not want.* I inhale deeply, bringing my cognitive responses back online.

Thinking. Yeah. Why is this guy making himself comfortable in my room? What is he doing in here? I clear my throat. I've got to get him out of here. "I'm Arden. But look, there's no party up here. Just boringness. You should probably make a U-turn." My words sound convincing, but I can't keep my eyes from grazing his body. Slowly. "I'm sure they're all missing you downstairs." *Or at least the girls definitely are.*

"No, I doubt they even know I'm gone," Devin cocks his head to the side to take in the blue and purple papier-mâché moon mask I made when I was nine. I watch his back rippling underneath his black shirt as he shrugs. "I doubt anyone down there even knows my name. That's the thing about house parties, right? They're made up of a bunch of people who barely matter to each other. Like a temporary ant hive—the mass is more important than one individual." He chuckles. "Or at least it feels like that." He brushes light fingertips along the lips of the moon mask. "I'm not all that interested in parties, to be honest. They just feel so repetitive—like, it's just the same scenes of meaninglessness over and over. I'm more into one-on-one connections," he says, turning toward me.

I make the mistake of looking up into his eyes. Like that, I'm sucked into another otherworldly vision. This time we're laughing and holding hands, sitting in the grass, watching fireworks going off in a backyard. The experience is so real, I can hear the booms echoing and smell the burned sulfur in the air around me.

I tear my gaze away from Devin's and find myself back in my room, holding my desk chair for balance. *Am I on drugs?* No, I assure myself after careful thought, I have not ingested anything out of the ordinary. I've been in my room, avoiding my sister and her party, trying to write. *Is Devin doing this to me? Am I doing this to me? Every time we lock eyes, I see, what? His thoughts? A scene from the future? Could I be reading his mind?*

"So, what do you like to do, Arden?" he asks.

I shiver hearing the way he says my name. Like it's a precious, magical word. *This is intense.*

"I like to read and write," I say softly, looking at my hands. "I'm pretty uncool, as my sister loves to remind me. She's the social butterfly of us two. You know, I should actually go check on her," I move to the left but Devin steps in the same direction, swallowing the gap between us. Now we are nearly touching. Our chests move in sync. I am consumed by the heat radiating from his body, the scent of fresh laundry and rain. *He smells so good. This is so bad.*

"There's nothing uncool about you, Arden," he says in a tone of deep prayer.

I take a tiny step backward and see his eyes focusing right on my lips. I hear his voice like a chant, "I'm going to kiss her. I've found her. I'm going to kiss her," but his lips are unmoving. *I'm hearing his thoughts. Oh, shit! This is actually happening.*

My gaze falls to the rug, the familiar mermaid shapes somehow grounding me as my mind darts wildly. *Reading minds? What is this ridiculousness?* Okay, I've always been able to get a sense of people, to gauge their feelings from body language or tone. But this sensation? This is completely different. I am reading his mind. I am feeling his feelings. When I look in his eyes I am seeing—what? A premonition of us?

I have never felt something this intense in my life. Why am I able to connect with him like this? What is going on with me? Backing away from Devin, I nearly trip over my desk chair. *Mermaids. Think of mermaids.*

"Are you okay?" he asks.

"Yes!" I lie, staring at the carpet. "No, actually, I'm not feeling okay," my voice wavers. "I think you should leave." I follow the waves that circle the rug, and I catch Devin in my peripheral, shoving his hands in his pockets.

"I'll leave you, I promise. It's just . . . Please don't freak out, okay?" He draws a deep breath. "I knew we were going to meet tonight. I've been dreaming of you for weeks."

"What?" I glance at Devin's face and hear him think, "I have to get her to believe me." I look down again as he holds out his hands.

"Look. This is a pretty wild story, but it's the absolute truth. I know we don't even know each other, like at all. I know we just met for the first time tonight. But . . ." He drops his hands and turns his face toward the ceiling. "Ugh! This is going to sound so weird! Probably because it is so weird. But the absolute truth is that I have been seeing you in my mind, seeing these scenes of us together, constantly, for weeks. I thought I was losing it. Like seriously, I went to the doctor for a CAT scan. But then I met your sister at the mall today. I nearly had a heart attack seeing her face in real life."

I watch him flex his hands, the muscles swelling and falling. I have to remind myself to breathe as he turns toward me. "She told me I should come to her party and I thought, okay, I'm finally getting to meet my dream girl. I had no clue you two were twins when she invited me. She didn't even tell me her name!" He steps closer, "But when I got here, it was clear she wasn't the girl from my dreams. But still, I could *feel* that you were here, in this house somewhere. I followed that feeling to this room, and I knocked, and I found you. It is you I am destined to meet, Arden."

"What?" I whisper, my mouth dropping. Devin's story is absolutely bananas, but . . . maybe *some* of this make sense? Who sent him these future visions in the first place? Is there some psychic cupid at play? He *felt* me in the house? How the heck does that work? I run my hands through my curly hair and breathe out heavily.

I look up into Devin's dark brown eyes again and I know he's completely sincere in what he's seen and what he feels. I absorb his excitement and nervousness. His want for me travels from his body into my own like waves in an ocean. "This is so intense!" his thoughts whisper loudly. "I didn't think she was real, but she is, and she's incredible."

He's thrilled to finally be with me. Me!

"God, I have to kiss this girl." The words travel through his mind just before it happens. His arms grip my waist; my arms slide around his shoulders. I feel like I might melt into a puddle. His lips come closer.

"Arden?!" Aurora bursts through the door, barefoot, wobbling, her face struggling at the intersection of anger and drunken abandon.

I nearly laugh at the state of her. Her black, one-shouldered mini-dress is half soaked against her body. Her hair looks electrified, shocked out of a loosely-held bun. But her eyes are blazingly alert as she takes in the room.

"Don't people knock in this country anymore?" Devin asks as I push away from him.

"What are you doing in here with my sister?" she demands, her words slurring around a thick tongue.

"Aurora, just calm down," I say, shaking my head at the vomit between her toes. "You're a mess."

"Yeah, take it easy. It's not like there's anything illegal going on here," Devin shrugs.

"Oh really?" Aurora steps to him. "We're not eighteen yet. I've been asking around, and you're nearly twenty-two, right Devin?"

"You're twenty-two?" I definitely didn't see that in his mind.

"Yes, well, I'm twenty-one, actually," he says.

I guess it's not too much of an age difference, but Aurora seems intent to kill this scene, one way or another.

"You did realize this was a party for our eighteenth birthday, right?" Aurora digs. "Freaking pedo."

"Look," Devin says, "I realized this party is for your eighteenth birthday after I was already here. I'm not . . . I wasn't trying anything other than to meet the girl I keep dreaming about. Arden, I should have told you my age earlier. This has all messed with my head, but this . . . this thing between us . . . I'm willing to wait for you. I don't want anything but a chance to show you that you can trust me."

I'm transported through his eyes in the next moment, and I see his dreams of us—laughing at a movie, playing in the snow, having a picnic, adopting a spotted pit bull at the pound. In a moment, the vision clears. "We get a dog?" I whisper.

Devin laughs. "You can see the visions, too? This is what I've been telling you!" He pulls me into an embrace but Aurora flies between us.

"No, no, no! You can't come in here acting all hot and heavy with me at my own party, and then just walk upstairs and move on to my sister, spouting some PhD-level creepster crap about your destiny."

Ah! Now I get it! Aurora wanted him first.

Aurora stamps her foot. "I say no!" Her voice cracks as she lunges for a final wild shove but misses, nearly falling on her butt.

"Aurora, nothing happened," I say, but she turns her face away from me. I decide to focus on her mind. *Aurora, we were only talking*, I plead. I try flipping the mind reading in reverse, transmitting my thoughts to her. *I was just coming to get you*, I pulse with my mind, my heart, my body. But as her eyes blaze between me and Devin, I feel the message getting rejected, bouncing backwards as if there is a fire wall between the two of us. I grunt at the magical rebuffing. Aurora has been blocking me out all day, so it figures I can't transmit my thoughts with her now. "I didn't even know you were interested in him!" I say aloud. "I'm sorry!"

"Forget it!" Aurora stamps her feet. "There is no need to lie, dear sister." Her eyes turn coldly on me. "Honestly, I'm impressed with your newfound interest in men. Let's give Arden a round of applause! She finally managed to look up from a book!" She slow claps and walks in a circle around Devin and me, taunting us. "And you had him in here all to yourself without any assistance? For like, what, a whole hour? Well done, sister. I couldn't be prouder of how you've grown. Maybe you're not such a bore after all. Maybe you're just a whore in disguise, is that it?"

So, I have never had a rage blackout in my life. But my hand is already back to me when I realize what the sensation of my stinging palm plus the shocked look on Rora's face indicate: I just slapped her. *I just slapped my sister!*

"Oh my god, Aurora!" I screech. "I'm so sorry! I don't know what happened!"

"Aaaah, I'm going to murder you!" Aurora screams, launching herself at me. She charges me to the ground, knocking the wind out of me. Devin reaches in to lift her off of me, but not before she gets a clean shot to slap my face. Hard. Devin pulls her arms back, but she leans in close to my ear and spits out, "I know you're not sorry, bitch." Then she bites my ear. I scream, pushing her shoulders away, digging my nails into her arms. But she's frantic and relentless. The moment I'm about to shove her off of me, she rebounds again with more energy. In a struggle to help, Devin winds up on the ground as well, his body half on top of me as a human shield from Aurora's wailing arms and legs. And at just that moment, we all hear a heavy stomp at the door.

"What is going on in here? Young ladies!"

I turn and see our godfather, Leo. *What is he doing here?* And whoa, is he mad. For good reason.

Leo squints in disbelief, taking in Aurora and me with Devin wedged between us. "What is this?! Get up from the floor, Aurora, Arden! Are you animals?" Leo growls. I have never seen him this furious, and I have known him my entire life. "I cannot believe what I am seeing! A house party? And who is this man in your room?"

Leo slaps his hands in anger, like he wishes he was slapping any one of the three of us. Aurora is breathing hard as we all get up from the ground. I wonder if she's going to hurl.

Devin steps forward. "I'm very sorry, sir. Things got out of control. This is my fault." Devin holds out his hand in contrition. Leo, however, looks right through him, focused on us.

"I'm speaking to you, Arden. Who is this man in your room? And why is he still here?"

"He's one of the guests, Leo," I smooth my hair with a shaky hand. "We just met. I didn't invite him. I didn't invite anyone."

"Way to throw me under the bus, bitch," Aurora sputters, reaching her hand around Devin, attempting another slap at me. I block her with my arm.

"Aurora!" Leo yells. "Is this how you speak in my presence? Are you intoxicated, girl?"

"Maybe," she says, indignant as ever.

Leo turns his shaking head away from her, pinching the bridge of his nose.

"I think it's best if I go." Devin squeezes my arm and whispers, "I'll see you again, soon."

I look away as Devin exits. Under the weight of Leo's piercing gaze and Aurora's jealousy, I feel overwhelmingly guilty. *I will put him out of mind*, I tell myself with zero conviction.

Then Aurora crumbles to the floor in a drunken heap.

"Come on, drunkie, stand up." I nudge her with my foot, and she grunts, unmoved.

Leo wipes his face with a handkerchief, then runs his hand through his pepper-gray beard. "As I see, you've been taking good care of your sister tonight, huh, Miss Arden?" Leo says, cutting his eyes on me.

I look down at my twin now playing with the fringe of the mermaid rug. At this point, taking care of Aurora would require a rope, a shovel, and a burial plot. I stand silently, waiting for Leo to ream Aurora out. But instead he continues staring at me, stewing on my face alone.

I shake my head as I realize the actual biggest frustration in my life. Having someone who looks exactly like me running around saying and doing things I would never, ever say or do, and then being implicated in the consequences.

"And how is your mother?" Leo asks me softly after a moment of eerie calm. I bite my lip once again, continuing the dunks in my bath of shame. I haven't even thought of Mom for hours. I thought about her earlier, but then . . . she dissolved from mind, buried deep under all this boy-min-dreading, sister-drunk drama. But Mom . . . yeah. She would have landed already. A while ago, actually. She's probably with the opera right now. I scratch my head as I calculate the time difference.

"She landed earlier, right? I'm sure she's swamped and will call us soon from the hotel." I smooth my hair.

"Oh really?" Leo's eyes squint at me. "What if she had been trying to call you just now? Like you would hear the phone through all the partying and wrestling with boys? Why do you think I'm standing here? I've called you both about a thousand times this evening! You don't even know what's going on with your mother!" He's breathing heavily now, his voice close to tears. "Something has happened."

"Oh god, Leo. What's wrong?" I grab his arm and find

myself immediately sucked into viewing the last hours of Leo's life. I see him yelling into the phone. Dialing my phone number while running to his car. Screaming a voice mail to Aurora as he speeds on the freeway. I feel Leo's confusion, panic, and desperation. I gasp at the crushing fear as I receive the phrase "mortal danger." *Mom is in mortal danger.* In a flash, I am back in my bedroom, holding Leo's arm.

"Your mother is missing," Leo says evenly, covering his cold hands over mine.

"What?" I shake my head, rejecting his words. "No. No."

But Leo nods, "Yes, I spoke to the police in London. She's been missing for hours." He takes a jagged breath. "She exited the private plane at Heathrow and then just vanished. Vanished! There is security footage showing her exiting the plane, but then she disappears behind a blind spot. The opera, the hotel, the chauffeur—no one has heard from or seen her!"

"She's probably just shopping or sightseeing," Aurora, still a heap on the carpet, slurs through her fog.

Leo sighs again, rolling his eyes at her drunken state.

"No," I say, contradicting our drunk oracle. "Mom wouldn't disappear without checking in with the opera first. She was so excited to be going back. This isn't her. This is bad."

Leo nods at me again. "Exactly. Selene might be less than respectful of time, but it's not like her to go missing on such an important night. She knows everyone is waiting on her. But the thing that makes this even more worrying is that the pilot reported she was extremely lethargic on the flight. They worry she's been taken somewhere against her will."

"She's probably just on an early honeymoon with our future stepdad," Aurora giggles and hiccups to herself.

"You think she was drugged and kidnapped by someone?" I deduce. "But who? Who would do this?"

Leo shrugs helplessly.

I stare into his heavy eyes and feel my consciousness slip into his mind. Maybe I can do this on purpose now? *Try to read his memory,* I say to myself, *to see what he knows.* I see a projection: Leo in his office. He's talking to the airport security, yelling and pounding his fist. "What do you mean, she's not showing up anywhere? How could someone disappear between the plane and the terminal? That's what I'm asking. Did someone working for your incompetent company kidnap Selene? Well, it appears someone on your team must have helped, and I want answers!"

"Of course we're hoping your mother is fine," Leo says out loud. "That this is all a misunderstanding, and she'll turn up soon. That's what I'm praying. But it's not looking that way." Leo's voice breaks, and he clears his throat thickly. "The London police are on alert and the opera has dispatched their own detective to investigate."

"What can we do to help?" I ask, my hands wringing of their own accord. *Mom is missing. Someone has kidnapped my mother.*

"The police are handling it," Leo huffs, shaking his head. "They say we should just stay put in case she comes back here."

"Ugh. I'm kinda not feeling so great again," Aurora scrambles from the floor and rushes to the bathroom connected to my room. Seconds later, I hear her retching.

Leo and I shudder at the sound. "I can't say I'm surprised Aurora wanted to throw a party in your mother's absence," Leo pinches the bridge of his nose. "But I'm disappointed that you let it—and her—get so badly out of hand."

"Me?" I tilt my head. "Are you seriously mad at me? I can't control Aurora. She doesn't listen to me. There was nothing I could do to stop her. She was determined to have this party!"

"Is that right? And I just wonder what you could do with some determination of your own?" He raises his brow.

I hang my head at the stinging comment.

Leo sighs and lays his hand on my shoulder. "Arden, you are one of most emotionally intelligent people I know, yet you underestimate yourself over and over. Of course you cannot control her, but you can love her more than anyone. If you want to help your mother right now, be there for your sister. She needs you, you need her, and yet here you are fighting each other."

He delivers these words with soft intensity. Even so, they land hard. He is right. I know my sister better than anyone. Something heavy is going on with her right now. She needs me, and I have to be strong for us both. And Mom . . . I had pushed aside my feelings about her trip, denying my sadness about her absence. Yet, I felt that stabbing ache in the pit of my stomach all day. I knew something was wrong. Now I know what it is. Mom needs us.

"Wherever your mother is, she needs you both safe," Leo says, embracing me. Everything suddenly clicks as his arms hold me still. Me, Aurora, and Mom. The three of us, standing, leaning together. We are like a triangle, each side holding up the other for balance. My sister needs my love, and our mother needs our help. Right now, the sides are scattered, and I have to make us whole again.

Leo's phone rings. He lets me go and glances at it with a groan. "It's one of the contractors I work with; I need to take this call." He walks downstairs, and I join Aurora in the bathroom, my head already beginning to swim with plans. And plans within plans.

"I'm pretty sure I need to pass out now," Aurora grumbles. Her head is in her hands as she sits on the side of the tub.

"No. You're going to wait on doing that. Do you know why? Because the night is not nearly over for us." I'm pacing the pink floor tiles, in full-on strategy mode. It's like I just overturned a 10,000 piece puzzle, and I'm itching to solve it—processing information, making connections, forecasting possibilities.

I'm not going to wait until this plays out badly. Aurora and I need our mother, and we have two options now: we can take the easy way and wait for news, or we can become active players in our own lives. We can take the hard way.

"What do you have in mind m'lady?" Aurora asks as she moves to the toilet bowl.

I smile, knowing she feels too horrible to put up a big fight against what I'm about to say.

"We're going to London to find Mom."

# 2

## *Aurora*

## UNDULATION

*A*rden is pacing back and forth in the bathroom, crafting *Operation Mom Rescue* in hushed tones. I've heard her crack her knuckles a dozen times, popping her fingers one by one. She won't stop moving her feet, her hands, or her mouth. Me? I'm here literally and figuratively failing to rise to the occasion. Yup. Action Packed Aurora! Now available to sit on the side of the tub while the world seemingly falls apart! Any movement beyond my eyeballs brings waves of nausea, though I have nothing left in my stomach but regret.

But honestly? I don't believe Mother is in danger. She's probably off being "spontaneous" or "free spirited," as she calls it. I call it unreliable. Arden is worked up over nothing. I mean, look at my twin—her cheeks flushed, forehead glowing with perspiration like she swallowed poison and her system is losing the battle. If she doesn't calm down, Leo's going to have to take us both to the ER.

Leo. Our big-hearted, long-suffering godfather. He's the closest thing we have to an actual father, and he sounded like he wanted to knock our skulls in just now. This must be the worst day he could ever imagine. He's been in our life since the beginning, tutoring us half the year wherever we were stationed, vacationing with us during Mother's down time. He always makes himself available to do anything Mother asks, and I see the look he saves just for when Mother laughs. I'm convinced he's been in love with her forever. It's no wonder he's gone berserk because she hasn't checked in with him or us.

But it's all going to be fine. I don't get why we should assume it's something sinister this time. Mother is just being flighty. I bet she lost track of time shopping. Or decided to escape with some fans on a getaway. She has missed many important moments in the past due to romances that consumed her focus and energy. She probably met a man on the plane and decided to follow him to his hotel.

Or, and I wouldn't put it past her because she loves pulling petty moves, maybe Mother is paying me back for being pissed at her for leaving this morning. Like, icing us all out, making us all worry, just to prove she's in control. Oh, I bet this is what she's up to! This is so her style, passive-aggressive as hell. She gets to punish us, have her fun, and then pretend she's all peace, love, and togetherness when we confront her. There's nothing wrong with Mother. She will turn up any minute with a lame explanation. She's perfectly fine, doing whatever. As she always does.

So, THE DEAL with our mother? She's an opera singer. A very famous one. The kind who gets bombarded in public by fans, who has a whole team to coordinate her movements and demands. Selene, first name only, was discovered when she was just a young girl, plucked from a Jamaican orphanage to train with the best voice coaches around the globe. After a successful début, years of touring followed, along with albums and even some movie musicals. When she got pregnant by one of her many lovers, she refused to name him or to slow down. Instead, she continued, bringing her twin girls along as she gobbled up fame and success like a Hungry Hungry Hippo.

Thus Arden and I grew up bouncing across the globe. We were tutored from box seats; we lived out of suitcases in various hotels and homes of friends of a friend. We played backstage with ropes and pulleys and learned to apply lipstick and eyeshadow from the opera's own makeup team. Cities morphed from one to another, but the theater was our home. The crew was our family. And our mother was the star around whom everyone orbited, including Leo. We created our own universe from what remained constant, which was each other. Everything else seemed to slip away just as I touched it, like a fistful of sand held underwater. We were experts at adaptation before we understood the word.

Arden and I were sixteen when Mother took a sabbatical to lecture at the University of Cincinnati in Ohio. We settled into a home for the first time, ever. It was then that my life as Aurora, not just one half of Selene's twins, really began. The teen culture in our suburb fascinated me, like a chess set I want to master. I was ignited by the social scene that develops when you stay long enough to actually be a part of the picture.

Unlike Arden, who hid in her stack of fantasy books, I

built friendships. I collected plenty of enemies along the way, too, but honestly, they only made the landscape more intriguing. I went out on proper dates here, and I came to realize there's really nothing about the guys themselves that keeps me at it. What I'm interested in is who I am with them, who I get to discover inside of me when I'm dating a new guy, who I transform into in front of a captivated audience of one. I like uncovering new sides of me—how I can be flirty or mysterious or vulnerable or dismissive. I date them to find out about me. I guess when you think about it, they're basically just mirrors who pay for the tickets to where I want to go.

Anyway, so when Mother wanted to get back on the road after a year, I refused. I didn't want to give up my normal teenage life—the discoveries and freedom. I demanded we stay put. I said that Arden and I should be allowed to finish high school with our class. Arden mostly stayed out of the weeklong screaming fest that resulted in a standoff. She did interrupt a silent dinner on the eighth night to say that staying put for a few years wouldn't end Mother's career, not unless she wanted it to. After that evening, Mother conceded. She promised no trips, no performances, just family, for an entire year. A month later, she publicly announced her retirement from touring, though her statement left room for her to change her mind. Since then, things in our household have been calm, predictable, boring. Midwest basic, if you will. We've had months of actually getting along. That is, until our mother up and decided to abandon us before our biggest birthday. Because what is family compared to the glittering stage?

.ౚఎ.

I MASSAGE MY temples, willing my sister to stop talking. I know I can't open my mouth without throwing up, but I can't hear this anxiety spiral anymore. My head feels like it's been hijacked by a tiny construction crew. I belch, and my mouth fills with the thick taste of licorice. Ugh. That would be the Jaeger. Those bombs probably weren't the greatest addition to a night of keg stands, Jell-O shots, and rum and Cokes. Closing my eyes, I beg the universe to remind me to never drink again.

Even if I weren't drowning in an ocean of alcohol, I still wouldn't be spinning in a wild state of worry over Mother. I know she wouldn't worry for us. I've known it since Arden and I were seven and we spent a few months living in the Bahamas. My memories of that time are filtered by the bright sheen of sun, sand, and ocean. Mother was performing on a luxury cruise ship. Leo was off somewhere, building his architecture empire. Arden and I practically lived outside near the water. Mother called us "beach babies" and joked she was going to send us off to be raised by mermaids. We had just learned to swim, which opened up a whole new universe. While Arden preferred playing in the sand, building sandcastles or digging for the center of the Earth, I was enticed into the clear water and undulating waves.

One day, as I was swimming in the ocean, I got lost in the feeling of my body gliding so easily in the water, in rhythms of breast stroke and back stroke. Before I knew it, I was out so far I couldn't see the shore in any direction. The ocean floor became a dark mystery below me. In a panic, I forgot how to swim. I splashed like an injured seal, yelling for Arden and Mother. My mouth filled with salt water. The sun blinded me. My body getting tired and weak, a chest-seizing terror trapped me. I was going under.

Then suddenly, I felt strong arms wrap around me, lifting me upward, keeping me afloat. Too exhausted to open my eyes, I clung to the warm, curvy body that moved me swiftly through the water. *Mother*, I thought. Who else would save me? Who else would hold me with such care? *I knew my mommy would save me,* was my final thought before I passed out in her arms.

When I came to on the sand, Arden was the only one there. She was frantic, shaking me.

"Aurora, are you okay? Can you hear me?"

I nodded, coughing as I slowly sat up. "Where is Mom?" I said, my throat burning with sea water.

"I don't know. But are you sure you're okay?"

"Mom carried me out," I said.

"No, it was someone . . . a woman I've never seen before. With long hair and skin so dark, it looked like midnight. She pulled you to shore, then she disappeared into the water so quickly, I couldn't even say a word. But I'm just glad you are okay!" Arden embraced me tightly, and behind her back I looked out into the ocean, wondering who it was that rescued me.

Because it certainly wasn't my mother. When I needed her, she was focused on her romance with the cruise director. Later, Arden and I found her giggling with him under a canopy. I will never forget how she turned to us and flippantly said, "Oh, you two. You're having fun and staying safe, right? Good." Then she turned right back to snuggling the cruise director without waiting for us to respond. Because she didn't actually care if we were all right or not.

Neither Arden nor I ever told Mother about the near-drowning incident. We just agreed that since I was fine, we would move on. But I've never quite moved on. At that moment I stopped calling Selene anything but Mother. No Mommy or Mama or even Mom—I felt they were too soft, too intimate. Too much of a reward. If Selene can't even see me and save me when I'm drowning, if she is more concerned with her affairs than her children's lives, then she doesn't get to be Mommy.

So now, even though Arden is set to play Rescue Rangers, I didn't see why we should. First, Mother wouldn't do the same for us. Second, there are scores of trained professionals already on the case, if there even is a case. And third, okay, by the time we could sneak away from Leo and board a flight to London and start looking for her, Mother could very well be on her way back home. It doesn't make sense!

I sigh heavily at the internal combustion engine that is Arden pacing the floor, wearing it into a fine dust. She flings her curls away from her face with a level of aggression I know the curls did nothing to deserve. She continues mumbling to herself, her voice rising and falling in intensity. Tears fall from her cheeks onto her shirt.

Oh, crap. I hate seeing this. Yes, I pick on her all the time, but I don't like seeing my sister cry. She's easy to give her love but also easy to break when that love is not returned. To see her crumbling over this makes me want our mother here, right now, so Arden can be okay again. My twin needs our mother more than I ever have or will. It's easy for them to vibe on each other. I'm not even mad or jealous about it; it's just one of those truths about my family. Mother and I are clash and friction; she and Arden are a symphony. I think I'm more like our father. That is, I make the assumption that I'm like my father, even though I have no idea who he is.

That's right—we don't know who our father is. At all. We do know it's not Leo, but other than that, nothing. I know it sounds so pathetic, like, "Who's the baby daddy, waah, just do a Maury episode and get it over with like everyone else in America." And like, yes, I agree, I want the answers. I'm even willing to do a whole *Mama Mia* thing and track down this sucker. But you must understand this important thing: My mother has unshakable determination over just a few things in life, and she is determined that Arden and I will not know our father. It's like trying to squeeze juice from a brick; she won't help us search for him or share anything about him at all.

In Prague years ago, after she discovered I was asking the crew about who our father could be, she went livid, screaming at me, demanding I never speak of him again. I refused to respond, though her rage had me thinking she might slap me for disagreeing. I was ready to catch a slap if it meant she understood I was going to uncover my father, someday. Arden is fine not talking about him. She doesn't want to even try uncovering him. She's told me repeatedly to just let it go, to be grateful for what we do have with one another, with Mother, with Leo.

In so many ways, Arden's like the much sweeter version

of me. Seeing the bawling mess she has become since hearing Mother is missing makes me ache for her. Not to mention I have been garbage to my twin today. What is wrong with me? Why am I so on edge? *Maybe you can press pause on being terrible and useless for one moment?* I think, and gather the strength to speak.

"Arden?" I call out meekly.

She brushes me off with a wave.

"Arden!" I say, sharper this time.

She turns to me with a cocked eyebrow. "I know what you are trying to get into," she says, "but I already told you I didn't invite that guy into my room, and I don't want to talk about it right now."

"What? Who?" I ask.

"That Devin guy. The older guy. I was not trying to take him from you or whatever you think was happening, okay? I'm not trying to fight you over some guy." Arden crosses her arms at me.

"Devin," I echo slowly, the last hour coming back through bits and pieces. She thinks I'm still upset about the whole kiss/bitch slap situation? I'm already so over it, I barely remember it happening.

"Yes, Devin! His name is Devin," Arden says, rolling her eyes, resuming her pacing.

Does she really think so little of me to assume I'm stuck on that stupid boy drama? I watch Arden massage the tip of her ear. *Wait, did I bite her ear?* I really need to never drink again. "I know his name is Devin . . ." I begin but she cuts me off.

"You're ridiculous!" She whips around, her hands balled

into fists beside her. "I don't even know how you can still be concerned with him when we have bigger things going on! Or are you still too wasted to even notice I am trying to figure out how to save our mom? I don't know how to deal with you!" She sighs and lifts her hair off her neck.

*She* doesn't know how to deal with *me*? I feel the strong urge to yank that hair to get her to pay attention. Suddenly the bathtub faucet twists hard and water spews from the nozzle, startling us both. *What the . . .* I reach over and turn it off, puzzled.

I take a deep breath and turn toward my twin. "Look, Arden, I want to talk about Mother. About what we should do for her." I try to stand but think better of it when the room tilts sideways. I ease slowly back to the tub edge. "I didn't want her to go to London. You know how upset I was."

Arden rolls her eyes once again and turns away from me. "This is so *not* about you, Aurora," she sighs, moving her shoulders and neck, cracking them loudly. "Why can't you see that?"

My face fills with heat. My hands contract. I really want to grab her neck. *Hard.* As soon as that thought comes, a towel flies off the wall hook and lands on Arden's head. *Flying towels?* As Arden wrestles with the cloth around her head, I stifle a laugh. "If it's not about me," I quip, "we can make it about you and the twenty-five-year-old man in your room, since that's what you want to talk about."

"Oh my god! You're a broken record! First of all, he was twenty-one, not twenty-five. And second, but most importantly, our mother is *missing* in another *country*!" Arden shouts, finally freed of the towel and full of fury for me. "Can we just focus on that? Pretty please?" It's the angriest and most sarcastic use of "pretty please" I've ever heard, and it makes me want to bite her ear all over again.

"Oh, I could focus if you could get off my back. Can *you* do that, *pretty please?*" Anger surges through my body. I stand up, successfully this time, and face Arden, silently daring her to take the first shot. At that moment, a framed painting of a mermaid drops off the wall with a crash. The lights in the bathroom flash brightly then dim. Arden and I look around. *Is this room haunted?* The hot water, the towel, now the painting and lights—something happens every time I'm about to pop off on my twin. *Am I making this happen?*

I move slowly and pick up the painting gently, the glass shattered but still holding together in the frame. It's one of Mother's favorites, a beautiful indigo-haired mermaid with dark lilac skin, sitting on a rock jutting out of the ocean. The mermaid's midnight blue eyes stare unblinkingly back at me through the cracked glass, almost like she's waiting on me to make a decision. Then I swear I see her tail and hair move. I carefully put the picture back on the wall, the shattered glass still bonded together somehow. *Am I bugging out or is something going on inside me?* I turn back and see Arden close to tears again.

"How am I on your back, when you keep bringing up Devin to embarrass me? How many times do I have to say I don't want to talk about it?" Arden sniffles. "Tonight was terrible. I'm trying to keep it together, to figure out what we need to do next, but it's like you just want to watch me drown in it. Is this fun for you?"

"Arden," I swallow hard, my heart sinking. *Why do I suck so very much? Stop jumping into the evil twin vortex, Aurora.* "Of course, this isn't fun for me! Ugh, I'm so sorry you even have that thought. I'm so sorry about everything tonight."

"Really? Suddenly you're sorry? You bit my ear, psycho!" Arden grabs her still swollen ear.

"I said I was sorry about everything!" I bark defensively, hearing my tone a beat too late. *What is my damage tonight?* I sigh and face my sister squarely. "Look, I am seriously sorry. I got all heated and out of control. I could blame it on the alcohol, but I shouldn't have bit you. Though, you did slap me . . ."

Arden rolls her eyes.

I place my hands on her shoulders. "Okay, I'll keep it real. The bite was pure malice and super wrong. I'm really, really sorry. Can we get past it, please? I love you more than anything, and I want us to make up. You can slap me again if that will expedite the healing."

I turn and move my cheek closer and closer to her face until she is practically kissing me. She smiles and tries to hide it, but I hear her quietly chuckle, giving in, like I knew she would.

"Okay, yes," she sighs. "You've been a complete and total brat, but I guess I accept your apology."

I bounce on my toes in response, but she shakes her head.

"I reserve the option of revenge any time I see fit."

"My ear. Your name on it. I got it."

We embrace, and I breathe in the sweetness of coconut and almond oil from Arden's hair. Then I pull back to look at her still furrowed brow.

"And another thing," I say. "You're right. We have to go to London tonight, Ar. It's up to us to find Mother."

Honestly, I don't really want to fly to London, but it's the only option I can take. Arden is the most important person in my life, so I will journey with her to find the most important person in hers.

"You agree?" She wipes the tears from her cheeks, and her entire body lights up.

"Yes, I agree," I say, nearly convincing myself. "Who knows if the police or the PIs are actually doing anything? We're the ones with the most at stake. We should try whatever we can to get her back." When I need to, I can lie through my teeth. It's a talent I learned early. *Stare at Mother and tell her you're fine, nothing happened.*

Arden throws her arms around me, and I feel like I'm hugging a better version of me—the person I could be. I look over her shoulder at the cracked glass of the mermaid picture. I'm pretty sure I broke it when I was thinking about choking my sister. Am I becoming some type of super villain, fueled by my darkest wishes? *Aurora, you've always known the truth and now this is proof. Deep down, you're a monster.* The nausea returns like a tidal wave.

"This is going to be great, Aurora. I can feel it," I hear Arden say as I collapse beside the toilet bowl and vomit.

# 3

## Arden
### Body of Water

*A*urora is snoring lightly in the seat next to me while I fidget like a flea-ridden dog. I twist my neck and peek around the airplane cabin. Nearly every seat carries a bored, restless, or sleeping passenger. The recirculated air tastes stale in my mouth and dry in my lungs. I swear I can pinpoint the sensation of a foul virus weaving itself into my bloodstream. We have one more hour till we land, and I'm clawing myself from the inside. How is it that my twin can rest so soundly when absolutely everything is a mess?

I lift the window shade and look out at the dark blue ocean beneath us. It feels like a black hole that could suck us up at any moment. I have always hated flying, especially when the plane has to cross over a large body of water. "What if we fall out of the sky into the sea?" I once asked Mom on one of our many flights from one end of the earth to the other.

"Oh, don't worry, baby. The mermaids will find us and swim us to safety. They're my dearest friends," she winked and wove her fingers through mine. She held my hand throughout the entire flight, even during dinner.

Now my hands are knotted together in worry. Mom is in mortal danger. In my heart I know this is true. When I think about how I sent her off with a smile yesterday morning . . . I could have done something to prevent this, right? At least Aurora tried to get Mom to stay.

I look at the crescent moon-shaped marks my fingernails have carved into my palm, and I think of my second source of worry. Aurora is a horrible liar. I always know when she's trying to get something over on me. Her left cheek twitches when she's being less than honest, and it was twitching up a storm in the bathroom. While I'm grateful she decided to join me on this quest, I know she isn't truly concerned about our mom.

I don't know why she's still being so fake with me. But it's fine. For real. I don't even think she knows I'm on to her, so she can just stay in her realm of secrecy for all I care. I can tell something heavy is going on inside her, but for now, I can't play my role in the Aurora show. My only focus is on rescuing Mom.

The pilot's voice comes over the loudspeaker and announces we are nearing descent to Heathrow airport. I feel my anxiety lift slightly, knowing we'll be on land soon. I tune the captain out as my thoughts travel to Leo. He's probably having a coronary right now, on the real. He was already blowing a gasket over the house party shenanigans, and now we've gone and snuck out right from under his nose. I pull the window shutter closed and pray Leo understands that Aurora and I have to do whatever we can to get

Mom back safe and sound. Of course, we left him with a note, but I'm sure his brain will explode once he reads it. I mean, I'd never seen him as upset as he was when he found Devin in my room, and this is so much worse!

And Devin . . . I don't know what to think, about either the guy or our potent chemistry. Why are we so drawn to each other? What does it have to do with this sudden mind reading thing that's happening to me? Ugh! No! I can't think about that terrifying magical crap. I have one mission: Rescue Mom!

"HELLO, LONDON. HOW I barely missed you," Aurora mumbles as we emerge from the customs maze into Heathrow's bright and airy terminal lobby. I'm swimming in several layers of worry as people around us kiss their hellos, exuberant at seeing their loved ones again. My stomach aches for Mom to be here, safe and sound, to greet us, too.

"Let's just take a taxi and get to the hotel," Aurora says, frowning at a young kid running to hug his mother.

"We're going to find her, you know." I nudge her elbow as I tug on my backpack.

"Yeah, sure. Piece of cake in a city of a billion people," Aurora mutters, dragging her own pack across the floor.

"Look!" I turn to face her, refusing to let her negativity stand. "I know you're faking it, but can you try doing it better? We are going to find Mom, okay?"

"What do you mean, I'm faking it?" she asks slowly.

Oops. So much for keeping the charade a secret. "Aurora, come on. I know you were dropping fat lies about wanting to come here. You think Mom's just partying on the Thames or whatever, but I *know* she needs us. You don't care, and it's fine, because I care enough for the both of us. We're getting Mom back. That's what's happening. So get on board, all right?"

My *Braveheart*-level passion leaves Aurora slack-jawed. We stare each other down for a moment. Aurora moves her mouth to reply, when we hear voices shrieking in our direction, "It's them! Oh yeah, I know it's them. Finally!"

"Yo, twinsies! Over here!"

Before I can turn to look, Aurora and I are mobbed by two squealing strangers. I catch a whiff of fresh flowers filling the air as I'm nearly tackled to the ground by one of them, who embraces me so tightly she knocks the air out of my lungs. When the woman releases me to embrace Aurora, I finally get a quick look at these strangers. They are slightly older than my sister and me, early twenties I would guess, with dark bronze skin, bright alert eyes, and killer dimpled smiles. They are definitely sisters, and they are beautiful with their wicked-stylish, punk-inspired outfits and hair.

One of the sisters is lithe and tiny, her hair in glamorously neat, ombre violet braids with both sides near her ears shaved low. She wears fuchsia leggings, a black perforated sweater with bleach spots, and black work boots that look like they've been through several battles. The other sister is a tall, voluptuous Ruben muse, her ombre hair in blue, waist-length dreadlocks. She wears a highly shredded T-shirt dress worn open over a leather patchwork cat suit. I'm speechless taking them in. This is how they roll through the airport, casually walking on fashion fire?

"Ugh, excuse you? Get the hell off of me!" Aurora sputters, pushing away her bear hugger.

I choose to take a more diplomatic approach, assuming these ladies are just confusing us with someone else. "I'm sorry, but do we know you?" I ask, untangling myself from an aggressive embrace.

"No, you don't! Ha! But that and these bags are just a few of the problems we'll have fixed soon, love," the taller curvy woman says in a melodious British accent. She winks and her diamond eyebrow piercing flashes in the light. She reaches out to take my small duffle bag, but I pull it back.

"Don't be afraid of us, love! We're your cousins! Welcome to Londontown, twinsies," the smaller sister says, her voice a higher pitched version of her sister's. She bounces on the balls of her feet like she's preparing to take flight. She's built like a pixie—petite features on a petite body, with a tongue piercing that makes her words come out in a lisp. She's the most adorable woman I've met in quite a while. "The twinsies are in London, London meet the twinsies," she sings while dancing around us, her arms making graceful circles, her legs leaping easily though the air.

"Let's cut it with that twinsies thing, Lilo. It's about time you two showed up though, mates," says the taller young woman as she takes in me and Aurora. "As you can see, we're excited. We've been dying to meet you for ages, you know!"

I'm really loving her calming aura, like nothing could happen that would shake her out of her inner peace. I'm about to tell her she's mistaken when the dancing sister tries to take one of Aurora's bags. My sister holds them to her chest and steps backward.

"Cousins? No. You guys must be confused. We don't

have any extended family," Aurora says, trying to move around the women, but they box us in again.

"Or, could it be that your mother didn't tell you about your relatives?" counters the curvy sister.

"Oooh, secrets and lies," quips the tiny one, making jazz hands. "You two really need to unbelieve that whole orphan angle a-sap, you know?"

"Who are you? What do you know about our mother?" I ask cautiously, my heart beating fast. Mom's life story is widely known thanks to the internet. But my skin and brain are tingling. I have this weird, instant connection with these ladies, with their energy and dimpled smiles. Could we be related to them? How do they know about us when we know nothing about them?

"Your mother, Selene. So, we've never met her, of course, but we know she's powerful and talented, like all the women in our family," the pixie says, bouncing on her toes with a broad smile.

"A powerful and talented soprano?" Aurora huffs. "Everyone knows that."

"No, a powerful and talented *goddess*," the pixie corrects with a nod.

"Oh, okay. I get it now," Aurora says with a squint of her eyes. "You two are super stans of hers, right? You think her talent is beyond this world? Listen, our mother is not a goddess. She's just a normal human woman who happens to sing well. That's it. And for the record, we don't have cousins anywhere, but thanks for stepping into the role for five minutes. It was very convincing. Four stars." Aurora grabs my arm. "Now, my *actual* family and I are gonna go.

And P.S., your outfits prove you're trying too hard, so just take the L and leave."

"Wow, oh my goddess, that is so precious. You really don't know, do you?" the taller sister says. "Either of you? She never told you two any part of the truth? Ah, I'm so sorry!" She crosses her hands over her heart. "Look, I understand you're hesitant to believe me now, but if you are really serious about rescuing her, you have to come with us."

"What? Why?" Aurora's eyes widen. "Did you have something to do with her disappearance?"

"Of course not!" The smaller sister says with shock. "Goddess forbid! We're here to help. We wouldn't hurt our own family." She looks at me, and her sincerity hits me in intense waves.

"We are not your family!" Aurora sputters. "Who the hell are you actually?"

"Right! I'm Liberty, but you can call me Lib," says the taller sister, reaching out her hand to me. "And this one-woman show is my younger sister, Leolidessa. She goes by Lilo. And honestly, all we're here for is to help you find Aunt Selene."

"Okay, whatever." Aurora rolls her eyes and turns away from Liberty's hand. "I don't know what this is about, but I reject it, fully."

Lilo throws up her arms and embraces Aurora again. "You need a hug, right? That's what I'm hearing. Just sink into this lusciousness, new cousin. You know what, I bet you're hangry. We need to get you some food!"

"Let me go!" Aurora frees herself from her tiny attachment.

"I'm trying to let you know it's all going to work out. Family is here for you!" Lilo moves toward Aurora again, but my sister takes a huge step backward and hisses like an angry cat.

"Stop it, Lilo. She doesn't trust you're harmless," Liberty laughs and flips her teal tipped hair from her shoulders.

"So, you're our cousins?" I ask. "But do you know who has our mother? How did you find out she's missing?" I step closer to the sisters. "Our godfather, Leo, said the police are keeping the disappearance quiet since Mom's a celebrity and they don't want the press interfering."

"Look, we don't know everything about what's going on, but we know enough. Tomorrow we'll take you to someone who actually knows it all and can give you all the answers: our grandmother." Liberty stares directly into my eyes and smiles. I feel my blood pulsing through my veins and thumping in my ears. Looking into her eyes is intense, and after a beat I find myself pulled into a vision. I see Lilo and Lib dancing around a bedroom, singing along to a French rap song.

"We get to finally meet our cousins tonight!" Lilo cries out happily. The vision shifts to one showing the sisters when they are younger, teenagers sitting beside each other on the train, holding hands.

"Gran Gran said that we would meet them, help them one day. We have to just believe her that it'll happen when it's meant to happen, right? Until then, we'll just send our love to them, wherever they are," Liberty says, consoling her sister.

This is the best news in the last 24 hours. We have

cousins, and they're, like, super hyped-up British versions of Aurora and me, and they're here to help us find Mom. Heathrow jackpot.

"So, let me see if I got this. You're Aurora, and you're Arden, right?" Liberty correctly identifies us, and I nod. "Sorry my sis and I are, as you say, super hyped up. We're just juiced to finally meet you after all these years."

She smiles evenly, but I bite my lip in shock. Super hyped up? Wait, can she hear my thoughts?

"Oh, and yeah, I can hear your thoughts." Liberty winks at me.

*What?!* My eyes nearly fall out of my head as Liberty chuckles.

"All the women in our family have different powers. And since we're related, our powers have the ability to connect and transfer back and forth. I can mentally connect with animals, but not other people like you can. But I can hear your thoughts when I stare into your eyes. It's like between the female relatives of our family, we can share a bit of our powers when we're together. But wait, you guys are *twins*, so you can, like, hear her thoughts and she yours, like all the time, right? Can you send each other visions from miles away? I'm so curious, what else can you two do together?"

"Let's go, Arden." Aurora reaches out her hand for me, but Lilo takes the opportunity to finally snatch the bag from Aurora's other arm. She hops around the group in glee.

"You can't go anywhere now that you're here, you're here now and you can't go anywhere," Lilo sings, cradling and rocking the bag like a child.

"Look, I've had enough of this shit. I want my bag now!" Aurora stomps her foot in frustration and holds out her hand. The bag snaps from Lilo's grip to Aurora's.

"Wait," I look back and forth between Aurora and Lilo. "How the hell did you get that bag, Aurora? Lilo, did you throw it to her?" Neither answers or even looks at me. "What is going on, Aurora?"

"Oh, you get out of here!" Liberty claps her hands together. "Okay, I could see not knowing *we* are goddesses, but you don't even know about *each other's* powers?!"

"Secrets and lies! Secrets and lies!" Lilo sings once again, grinning and bouncing on her toes.

"Did you *make* that bag jump to you?" I grill Aurora, but she just avoids my eyes.

"Mysterious powers and magical relatives. Everything is so fresh. Everything is so new," Lilo sings slowly with her eyes closed.

Aurora snaps at her, "How did you even know we'd be here tonight? Huh? If you two are really our cousins, how have we never ever heard of you?" She clutches her bag. "Why are you pestering us, and what does any of this have to do with finding our mother?"

"Such a temper and so very many questions!" Lilo mimics a mean face.

"Yes, because I want answers," Aurora snarls in reply.

"Oh, and I want one entire day with a completely lavender sky," Lilo sighs happily and resumes her dancing around the group.

"I promise we'll answer absolutely every question we can once we get to our apartment," Liberty says.

"There is so very much to catch you up on before you meet our Gran Gran. That's what she likes to be called, you know. Gran Gran. The Boss Goddess," Lilo says with an electrified full body wiggle.

"Oh, speaking of catch," Liberty says, taking a quick look at her phone, "we need to move to the Tube. Like right now."

I glance at Aurora, and she shrugs in defeat. "Fine, we'll go," she says, still avoiding eye contact with me. Always keeping her secrets safe.

Liberty nods and we take off, with Liberty dragging me forward and Lilo linking arms with a reluctant Aurora. We are swept through the bright airport to the subway, or the Tube, as the cousins say. It's a labyrinth; the walls change from glass to plaster to concrete to painted brick, the ceiling coming in closer and closer until we are bottlenecked onto a concrete platform, staring at an advertisement for the Tate Museum. Liberty smiles as we wait. Lilo is slowly moving her feet through the ballet positions. Aurora is fumbling with her cell phone. And I am trying my best to swallow the lump that has formed in my throat. So much of me is overwhelmed, but part of me is in celebration, as so many things click into place.

Aurora and I have powers. So that's what's going on with me. The visions? The reading of minds? Those things are really happening. Because I'm a goddess. I look at my hands, focusing on the lines across my palm as I etch the new facts into my mind. And Mom is a goddess. And she's in mortal danger because she was taken by some bad people who maybe also have powers? My hands tremble. There's nothing in them, but this all might be a bit too much to hold.

Lilo breaks the silence, chirping, "We have a guest room with single beds, and we have twin guests for the bedroom!"

In a gust of wind and lights, the train arrives, sliding through the tunnel like an electric snake. A looping, disembodied voice tells us to "mind the gap" as we step into the brightly lit, white and navy-blue train car.

We shuffle into a quad of seats, away from the crowded middle. Liberty and I slide our bodies and bags and sit on one side. Leolidessa and Aurora plant themselves across from us.

"Are you enjoying the fabulous experience of riding the London Underground? Isn't this just miraculous, twinsies? Look around you at all this splendor!" Lilo gestures about her at the bright train scattered with people, most of them looking at their phone screens.

"What splendor? We've ridden a subway system before. There's nothing miraculous about traveling like a mole," Aurora says, staring out the window into the dark tunnel.

As the train takes off, she gives everyone in sight a sour face. To make up for her malice, I smile welcomingly across the train and accidentally catch the eye of a lanky boy standing in the back. He is maybe fifteen, with longish greasy blonde hair obscuring his face. He's wearing enough baggy clothing to dress an entire football team. He shakes his hair out of his face and smiles back at me with a nod. I drop my smile, but it's too late. He's already begun moving toward us, making a path up the aisle, his young face more determined with each step.

"Oh no!" I hide my face in my coat. What is happening to me? I do *not* need another run in with a boy.

"What's wrong?" Liberty whispers next to me.

"I didn't mean to, but I think I might have given him the sign," I hiss.

"You flipped him the bird?!"

"No! I just smiled at him, but not really *at* him, but now he thinks I want to . . . Oh no, here he comes." I try to shrink myself into invisibility as the boy approaches.

"Hullo," he says in a thick British accent, moving a lock of hair behind his ear and smiling expectantly.

My face burns as I look into my purse for nothing, hoping he takes the hint.

"I, uh, I saw you looking at me, you know? And you're kind of cute I guess, yeah? I thought I'd maybe come over and maybe let you say hi to me, you know?"

"Ey, ey, sorry, sonny boy, no, no no. You are in the wrong space-time continuum right now, my man," Lilo barks at him, snapping her finger in the air. "This ain't no singles bar, not right here, not today. This is a train, love. We are trying to get to places you don't even know exist. My cousin, she ain't interested, you see. You gotta go."

"I . . . I just want to talk . . ." he stutters.

"No, no, you ain't saying nothing. Nothing!" Lilo gets up and pats him on the head. "Okay, how about you play a game, starting right here, right now. You never talk to a woman ever again. Your mom doesn't count, okay? But every other lady, you have no words for them, you got that? Now, go, young Kurt Cobain. Go!"

"But—" he starts in confusion.

"Eh! No words, remember? That's both the goal and the dream. You go now. Bye!" She gently pushes him back toward his end of the car, and, after a final sad glance at me, he shuffles away.

"Oh my god! Lilo, what was that?" I whisper at her when he is gone.

"That? That was me putting riffraff in its place, yeah. My cousin deserves a king—or a queen, if you like—but definitely not a scrub muffin. You didn't want to talk to him, I could see that. I got your back, Cuz!"

"Yes, but you could have been nicer to him about it!" I counter, still scrunched in the seat.

"Oh my god, here we go again with her niceness crap," Aurora grunts, rolling her eyes so heavily that mine hurt.

"There's nothing wrong with being nice, Arden," Liberty says. "But think about it. Nice won't get you or that boy anywhere in life. You could have tried to dismiss him politely, but he'd still think he had a chance and probably stalk us all the way home. Lilo was harsh, maybe, but he got the point that this love connection he was dreaming about wasn't going to happen."

"She told him to never talk to a girl again!"

"I know, I'm hilarious, right?" Lilo brushes off her shoulder. "Sometimes you gotta help people recognize their own limits, you know what I'm saying?"

"You mean crush their feelings?" I ask.

"No, he knows I didn't mean it, but next time he does talk to a girl, he'll try that much harder not to get shut down. He might even be presentable and charming and not just stand there blubbering because a pretty girl accidently smiled at him."

Lib nudges me. "You could send him that message directly."

"How?" I snort. "I'm so awkward around guys, I can barely talk to them."

"Oh, don't believe her. This one just had an older man eating out of her hand back home," Aurora snaps like a viper. No one acknowledges her.

"Use your mojo—your goddess powers," Liberty says, nodding her head. "You can do it. Speak to his mind. Let him know how he should approach a lady."

"What? I don't really know how to use my . . . mojo like that. When it's happened before, it's just me receiving visions of what others are thinking. It's mostly been by accident." I bite my lip, feeling embarrassed at all I don't know about myself and my powers. I hate the panic tightening my throat.

Liberty shakes her head and turns to me. "You got this, cousin. You just need to take control over your abilities. Concentrate on his eyes and listen with your heart to how he's feeling. Then when you're connected, think about what you want to say and how you want him to feel." She squeezes my hand and I hear her voice in my head, *You can do this, Arden. You can do amazing things. You're one of us.*

Right. I'm supposed to be this person who can overcome her own insecurities and do beyond great things. I can, at the very least, help this guy not feel like crap right now. I think over Liberty's words and what it means to be one of many great, powerful superwomen. This ability to influence another's emotions is a part of me. It's not an accidental thing. It's a me thing. So, I just have to be me. Sounds so easy.

I look toward the back of the train and find the blond boy sitting alone, earbuds in, hair in his face. I stare at him for quite a while until he feels my gaze. Finally, he looks up. Once I catch his eye, I don't let go, but allow his feelings to pour into me. The world stills as I absorb the sadness and embarrassment emanating from his darkened eyes.

"Hi, there. I'm sorry about all that. My cousin can be pretty blunt, but it was really nice of you to come over to say hello, and I should have said hi back. That was rude of me." I think these words. The wave of embarrassment recedes, but I still feel the sadness inside him, now inside me. It feels intensely lonely. My heart aches for him. "I know you're looking for love; we all are. I'm not the one, but when you find a great girl, you could compliment her, ask her questions, and be genuinely interested in her, and maybe the two of you will connect in a way that has potential for more." Instead of feeling loneliness, I now feel hope emanating from him. He's imagining meeting someone, what he will say to her, how he will start with a compliment, asking if it's okay for him to share a moment of her time. I blink and sever the connection between us. The train comes back into focus around me.

"Hey, Cuz," Liberty says softly. "You're back, right? What happened?"

"That was . . . I think . . ." I turn and look to the back. The boy is now bopping his head to his music, a wistful smile on his face. "I did it. I used my mojo. I gave him the message. It actually went well."

"Yes! Get it, cousin! You're brilliant! I knew you could do it. He looks well and chuffed now, right, Lilo?"

"Yes, look at him, like a less-wrinkled shirt. Not so embarrassing to look at. Steamed and definitely improved. He might talk to a woman again soon and not completely blow it next time. Can you imagine? Praise be!" Lilo waves her hands in celebration like she's sitting in church. "Isn't it just glorious how we change the world? Goddesses—saving men from themselves since the dawn of time."

"So, what does that really mean?" Aurora lowers her voice. "You, we . . ."

"What does it mean to be a goddess?" Lilo sings. "My dear cousin wants to know."

"All of the women in our family have these unique abilities and live for a long, long time," Liberty says with a proud smile. "Our powers were gifted to us directly by the Fates. We'll tell you the whole story later, once we get home, but yeah, basically we're not fully human. You're not fully human. We're all something more. We can do super awesome things in our family, and it's especially great when we're all together and able to collaborate and share our abilities. But even on our own, each of us is pretty incredible. You two won the family genealogy lottery."

"Welcome to the goddess club, twinsies!" Lilo says, shaking her head as if she, and only she, suddenly hears a techno beat.

"But, okay, how come I always felt completely normal? Like, I got the chicken pox. I've broken bones before. And I only just experienced my powers last night." I think of Devin's visions and can't help the heat that rushes to my face.

"Oh yeah, about that. Thank you so much for sharing

your burgeoning psychic abilities with me, dear Arden," Aurora sneers.

"Like how you explained that you can move things with your mind? That was a great heart-to-heart we never shared," I stick my tongue out at her.

"Hey kids, no scrapping on the Tube," Liberty clucks her tongue at us. "Gran Gran foresaw that your mom would suppress your goddess abilities from birth, to keep all of this a secret, so you would experience life as a regular human."

"Wow," Aurora says, sitting back and folding her arms. "What a flipping liar."

"Hey! None of that 'tude, missy, ya hear? Anyway, Gran Gran also saw that one day, Selene would make a hard decision to leave you two, and that decision would trigger your powers to return," Liberty explains. "And that just after that, we would finally all meet. Oh! We're coming up to our stop, ladies."

We gather our things and are told to mind the gap repeatedly on our way out. We follow Liberty and a skipping Lilo down a street lined with manicured gardens and cheerful houses. The sky is now a deep lilac with the setting of the sun.

"This sky! This is my favorite sky!" Lilo squeals, waving her arms in glee.

"Our building is just around here, but we actually really want to show you guys a little something first," Liberty grins.

"Is it another man child to fall in love with Arden?" Aurora snaps.

My face flushes with embarrassment.

"Maybe men can't help but be drawn to her pleasant

personality," Lilo answers in my defense. "You might know what that's like, too, Aurora, if you tried having one."

"Nailed it," Liberty squeals as she and Lilo slap high- and low-fives.

"There's nothing wrong with my personality," Aurora sputters, her eyes wide.

"You mean, that can't be fixed by a lobotomy?" Lilo supplies.

I choke on a laugh and Liberty covers her mouth, but we all hear her chuckling.

Lilo bursts into her signature dance, singing, "Aurora could use a lobotomy and then she'll smile at you and me," until Aurora lunges at Lilo, chasing her down the street into a park lined with trees, manicured lawns, and a smattering of colorful flowers growing out of thick bushes.

"Oh, watch. This'll be good," Liberty says as we walk behind them.

I have never seen anyone cut through Aurora's attitude like these two have. Since they found us in the airport, it's been a roast on Rora. It's literally a cause for celebration. Through the trees, I see the rippling reflection of the streetlights flashing on as the sun has nearly set. Liberty links her arm in mine. Our arms slide into place as if we've been connected for years. I hear the bubbling sound of running water as we approach a wooden bridge over a flowing creek. Arms still threaded together, Liberty and I lean forward to see the reflection of ourselves.

"You're beautiful, Cousin," Liberty smiles at my blurred reflection revealed by the water.

"Heh, thanks. Aurora and I got lucky in the looks department, I guess," I say shyly, turning away from my image. I never quite know what to say or how to feel after receiving a compliment. Especially about something I feel I had no hand in.

"No, you, Cousin. You, beyond your looks, are beautiful. Your sister looks the exact same way, but you can tell she's just overflowing with anger, like the world owes her something. But you? You just want to understand and love everything. You're afraid that your big heart makes you vulnerable, that you have to hide it away, but it's actually what makes you so beautiful." *I see it, clearly.* Liberty's voice says softly in my head. *How are you not able to? Huh?*

She nudges my ribs, but I just bite my lip and continue looking at the creek, ignoring my constantly shifting reflection. After a few minutes, Rora circles back to us, breathing heavily, a worried look on her face.

"I was right behind Lilo, but then she just disappeared. I yelled for her, but I can't find her anywhere."

"Yeah, I figured that would happen," Liberty laughs. "She most likely did something like this." In a breath, Lib's body begins to shrink and grow feathers. Her mouth stretches outward and hardens. Her long blue hair transforms into a feather tail.

Aurora and I stand frozen, watching Liberty finalize her silent metamorphosis into a small, navy-colored, teal-tailed bird that flies around our heads and begins to sing.

"What the hell is going on?" Aurora screams, but I laugh and clap my hands.

"Mysterious powers and magical relatives," I say, echoing Lilo's words.

In a moment Liberty is joined by another bird. This one is dark grey with a violet-colored streak down the center: Lilo. The two sister birds sing and dance around each other, flitting playfully over our heads. Aurora and I turn and turn, trying to keep up with their flight. They continue their song and are soon joined by five, then ten, then 20 or more birds who match their joy. I never heard anything like it before—a song melodic and lovely, like a community greeting. I want to cry from wonder as the birds join up to form the word "welcome" in the sky above the water.

"Wow!" Aurora says softly, breaking from her skepticism for a moment.

I nod in agreement. Our cousins are creative and loving and fearless. I'm overwhelmed to be their family. Lib and Lilo fly down and materialize next to us. The other birds flitter away into the night sky.

"How did you like your official welcome, twinsies?" Lilo asks, dancing around us, waving her arms. It's clear she's unable to confine herself to any single spot as either human or bird.

"That was absolutely amazing, beautiful, lovely! Just perfect!" I sputter. How do I explain that, watching them, I felt as though I completed a transformation, too? That watching them made me believe I can do amazing things, too? "You two are pretty incredible."

"So, but wait, you can both change into animals? At any time?" Aurora shakes her head in confusion, and I roll my eyes. Can't she just sit in a moment of appreciation? Why must we know how the magician performs the trick?

"It's actually Lilo's power," Liberty says with a slight

bow to her sister. "My special mojo is mentally connecting and communicating with animals. We've worked on our connection for a while and now, so we can share our powers when we're together. It helps us protect ourselves when we need it. And it means we can do cool stuff like put on a lil show to tell our cousins how excited we are to finally have them here." Liberty winks at me. "Anyway, we have a lot to tell you about our family and how you can control and grow your powers, back at our place. Tomorrow we'll go to Gran Gran, and she will let you know how to find your mother. We'll start strengthening and practicing your powers tonight. Or, right this very moment, if you're ready."

I nod immediately, one hundred percent more than ready to begin embracing the power within me. I've always been drawn to fantasy tales starring amazing heroines. Each time the heroine uncovers the magical destiny awaiting her, my heart races in excitement for the adventure ahead. As I remembered watching my cousins flying over the water, with no fear of falling or needing to be saved, I think of how they are their own heroines—goddesses in control of their fates. And they're telling me I'm capable of all of that? It seems like the whole universe has conspired to show me it's the perfect time to become my own heroine. This is my story. This is my time.

"Aurora?" Liberty asks. "Ready?"

Aurora nods slowly, full of hesitancy.

I feel I need to make up for her lack of enthusiasm, so I speak for both of us. "We're ready," I say. "Let's become goddesses."

# 4

## *Aurora*

## THEY NEED ME

*A*rden has been deeply secure in Sleepland for hours, but my jet lag has somehow been reabsorbed into my body. Even after an entire night of questions, answers, and power strengthening exercises with the cousins, I'm still not able to keep my eyes closed for a second. Electrified questions and answers continue to flood through my body, as if every cell has been jolted with lightning and I'm still buzzing from the surge.

How can I rest easy after hearing nearly everything I knew about my existence has been a lie? Arden snores softly in the bunk above me, while I'm staring blankly at the corner of the ceiling in my cousin's darkened guest room. I'm at war with a host of things I don't fully understand but desperately need to master.

Before landing at Lilo and Liberty's apartment, we stopped at a late night Chinese spot for take-out. Then, seated in our cousins' wood paneled living room, surrounded by containers and chopsticks, Lilo and Liberty began unravelling the story of our family.

So, apparently Gran Gran and our grandfather had five kids: four girls, all goddesses with a range of talents that connect them to the island and nature, and one son, Taresh, who disappeared years ago. He has no beyond-human abilities other than extended life. Liberty pulled out an aged black-and-white family photo that was taken in Jamaica, in the 1840s, by a French photographer. In it I saw a handsome black couple standing on the porch of a white, two-story house in a field, their five children gathered in the patchy grass in front. A shirtless teen boy, Taresh, crouched, staring aggressively at the camera. A girl around ten, our mother, beamed with a young toddler at her hip. Finally, two young girls, aged around four and five, clutched at the preteen's skirts, peering shyly at the camera.

Mother, we learned, is the eldest and most powerful of Gran Gran's daughters. She gave up most of her abilities in order to live as human, but the cousins shared what they know.

"Gran Gran won't talk about what she could do, your mother, but we know she was terribly gifted as a child," Liberty said in a whisper. "From what we've pieced together over the years, we think she could control water and manipulate emotions. Kind of like your powers, Arden."

"And her powers were amplified by the moon and sea," Liberty added.

Lilo and Liberty's mother, Martique, is next in line. She can control animals, like the cousins, but also weather and air. "Mom is wicked smart and doesn't put up with anything," Lilo said proudly. "She's the person you want around if there's trouble."

"Well, where is she now?" I interjected like a hostile prosecutor, leaning forward on the black leather couch. "Doesn't she care? You say you know for a fact that our mother has been kidnapped. Well? Where is dear Aunt Martique?"

"She's in Jamaica right now, and yes, of course, she cares. She's with our other aunts, on their own missions, living their lives, and keeping things together as only they can. I know you can't appreciate this now, but this?" Liberty pointed to the four of us with her finger. "We are the ones who need to be here, now, on this mission. We'll make an incredible force in getting your mother back safely."

"But how can you even say that when you don't know exactly where she is or who kidnapped her?" I slapped the couch cushion next to me, wanting to toss this whole four-way team into the nearest garbage heap. Of course, with my powers still being semi out of control, I sent a stack of magazines flying against the wall. Lilo, Liberty, and Arden looked at me measuredly, and I just knew they were thinking I'm the one most likely to blow this whole plan—a ticking time bomb at the very least, *a monster in goddess clothing.*

"I wish I knew who kidnapped her or where she is right now," Liberty said. "I don't, but I do know we'll figure it out together because Gran Gran told us so many years ago that this is how it would be, how it needed to be, to get your Mother back to us all. I can say it because Lilo and I are more than ready to do whatever we can. We've basically been training all our lives for this very moment. I can say it because look at your twin. Arden is charged up and ready to launch."

Arden nodded, cracking her knuckles like a boxer moments from the fight. I rolled my eyes. Ever the eager student, my sister. *The good one—leaving me to be the bad one.*

I figured that was all she was going to say, but after another long pause, Liberty cocked her head at me and says, "And you're nearly there."

I scoffed. Who gave her authority to judge me so casually?

"I know, but, really, you are! Your true self is in there, all right. But it's like we need to untangle all the crap you're wrapped up in, like unwrapping a mummy or something. But you're definitely in there. You're one of us."

"The worst of us," Lilo muttered underneath her hand, but I heard her clearly and marked this as the five hundredth time I have wanted to punch her solidly in the mouth.

"Our Aunt Victoria is next oldest," Liberty continued. "She has abilities over the earth and metal manipulation. She's so funny and tells the absolute best stories about her life. She's actually the one who will tell us things our Mom or Gran Gran don't think we should know. She also makes this gorgeous jewelry, like these," Liberty and Lilo held up their quartz necklaces, "and she fills them with protection and healing and cloaking powers for the wearer." As Lilo rubbed the purple stone, it shifted colors and glowed from within, pulsing as if awakened by touch.

"Wow, those are beautiful," Arden said, swallowing a mouth full of shrimp fried rice.

I nodded and stuffed my face with noodles. The powers, the pictures, the jewelry—it was hard to deny this fantastical story in the face of all this evidence.

"And finally, there's Aunt Larissa," Liberty said. "She's a healer, and she has the ability to communicate with plants. She's pretty quiet and keeps to herself. But if you're around her enough, she might open up to you and teach you some amazing things."

LYING SLEEPLESS IN bed now, I accept the fact that Arden and I come from a long line of baddies, that our mother is a goddess, and we are, too. But how did all this goddess family stuff even get started? Well, to say the story is surreal would be an understatement, but Lilo and Liberty swear this is how our family came to be.

It all started over two hundred years ago. The Fates, along with a group of elder Celestial Beings, had been envisioning and weaving the lifelines of every soul on Earth for eons. One day, they all got bored and plotted to basically make their own reality TV show. They decided to choose one couple on Earth and send them challenges. They would hide the couple's futures from themselves so watching them in real time would provide the maximum entertainment. Together they would view this couple and bet on how they would deal with circumstances and who they would evolve into over time.

The Fates quietly chose Gran Gran, or Ghani, and our grandfather, Ezekiel, a young, freshly married couple in a small parish in Jamaica. Ezekiel and Ghani were deeply in love, having known each other since they were just kids. Ezekiel was strong and smart, and very protective of his love, Ghani. Ghani was beautiful, witty, and kindhearted.

Together they laughed and talked from day to night, planning the beautiful life and family they just knew they were destined to have together. Unfortunately, things did no go as they had hoped.

The Fates sent them sickness, hurricanes, temptation, riches, destitution, drought, you name it, but the couple weathered every challenge, becoming stronger together. Their first child, a boy they named Taresh, suffered from many ailments and barely made it through his childhood. Despite their many troubles, they remained a tight family, grateful for what they had.

When they reviewed the footage, the Fates and Beings saw that Ghani was the spine that truly held the family and even their entire village upright. She was resourceful and determined, sassy and kind, loyal and loving. She was their favorite character to watch. As the years slowly passed, they decided to reward her for who she had become. They made her a Seer, giving her the discernment of souls, or the ability to read a person's life force and receive visions of their life, past, present, and future. The Fates and Beings also gave Ghani premonitions of the future and threw in direct access to communicate with the Fates on occasions, just to round out the prize package.

Apparently it went something like this: One day, Gran Gran was your normal kick-butt Jamaican mother and wife, then the next day she woke up supercharged, calling out liars, seeing crimes before they happened, and able to go into trances to receive downloads of information from the Fates and Celestial Beings. Ghani suddenly became a superhero. At first, she used her newfound gifts to bless everyone she met. People came from all around to visit her. They carried their problems and prayers, but also their jealousy and ill will. Ghani became famous and beloved throughout the island, but secretly a force was building against her.

Many men of the parish and beyond felt threatened by the celebrity and power of a woman, mother, and wife. When rumors surfaced of plots to execute Ghani, she brushed them off. Her husband Ezekiel was publicly supportive of his wife and threatened anyone who would plan to harm her. But slowly, Ezekiel fell prey to the persuasive nature of evil. He felt he had less and less of a role in society. People who used to come to him for help and advice now only wanted to speak with his wife. Like rot, jealousy and resentment set into his heart. In secret, he began to agree that there was something wrong with a woman who had too much power.

When Ghani became pregnant again, things started to go sideways at home. Ezekiel began showing his true colors. While Ghani prayed for a healthy baby, the Fates and Celestial Beings were angered to see Ezekiel demanding from the gods another boy, this time a gifted, strong son who would make him proud. His heart yearned for Ghani's powers and growing prestige, and he viewed the new child as his chance for prominence. He figured he could easily control this youngest child and eventually manipulate the abilities of both the child and Ghani.

The Fates and Beings were, rightfully, disgusted by so many things about this turn in Ezekiel's character. They hated his delusions of grandeur, his self-centeredness, and his sexist assumptions. They were sick of the patriarchy demanding to win. So they decided the child would most definitely have to be a girl. But not just any girl—a child beyond human, one blessed with the eternal gifts of the gods and goddesses. (I really like this part of the story. I imagine them standing around, open-mouthed, while Grandfather spouts some patriarchal mess, and then looking around like, "Oh hellz naw," and rolling up their sleeves.)

The Fates and Beings magicked up a child who, while made of human flesh, was also a goddess in her own right. They connected her power to nature and the island as a way to ensure she would have a recharging force while living an eternal life. While they gave power to the baby inside her, they gave Gran Gran some eternal life juice, too, making them both beyond human. Goddesses.

The Celestial Beings hoped Ezekiel's heart would change, that this child's talent would bless the world and the man and put Ezekiel's wishes for a boy to shame. They hoped he would be won over by his daughter and melt into becoming a better man for her, as many fathers do. But instead, Ezekiel shunned his daughter as she grew, becoming particularly cruel when she started to display her powers as a child. He told Ghani the next baby would have to be a boy. But over the years, the couple had three more girls, every one of them goddesses blessed with unique and enviable talents. Ezekiel spiraled more and more, becoming verbally abusive after nights out drinking, now openly supporting the mob who would overthrow his wife and daughters' power in the community.

After a heavy week of binge-drinking with the Women

Hater's Club (as I decided to name them), Ezekiel started thinking up his own plot against his wife. He thought if he got rid of his daughters in what looked like an accident, his wife would turn her backs on the Fates and her powers, and things could go back to the way they were before. He figured, if the Fates were responsible for his daughters then his daughters should be sent to live with them.

A few nights later, he snuck a heavy sedative in the family's dinner. Late that night, as Ghani slept, he loaded his four girls into a wheelbarrow and rolled them to the river, to a steep trail by a rocky waterfall, where he intended to dump them into the water, leaving them to drown.

So, this is where the story gets fuzzy. Apparently, the way Gran Gran tells it, the Fates saved the children from drowning. But according to Lilo and Liberty, the way Aunt Victoria tells the story is that our mother, Selene, stopped grandfather from killing his daughters at the waterfall by commanding the water to create a chain around grandfather's body, holding him back while the girls ran away.

Back at home, the Fates awoke Ghani and downloaded on her all that had occurred, including their decision to strike Ezekiel dead that morning for his attempted crime. But Gran Gran pled to them for his life. She knew he had been turned against her because of her powers, and she believed that one day she could get her husband back. She begged that he be given a chance to change. So the Fates decided Ezekiel would live eternally with his wife, but with no abilities beyond immortality. Then Ghani begged that the whole family could remain intact throughout time. The Fates relented, granting immortality to Taresh as well, but without the strength and abilities Ezekiel so craved. This would be Ezekiel's punishment: to never have the son he desired. He would live to see his wife and daughters and granddaughters grow ever more beautiful and more powerful than him. The Fates hoped that, throughout time, he would appreciate the bountiful gifts of his life and family.

Now, this was where I couldn't help but yell out, "Wait, if Gran Gran's such a soul-reading super goddess, why would she defend some attempted baby-killing loser, even if he is her own husband?"

"You have no idea what you're talking about!" Liberty reprimanded, grabbing my hands and shaking them. "This was a human man who found himself corrupted by the forces that prey on human men. Gran Gran believed that he could change, that there's always a chance for people to change for the better. I mean, imagine what they had already been through together. And now she was growing, evolving so much, and that change came with a backlash against the one she loved the most."

"Psh. Sounds like a lot of justification for domestic abuse," I muttered, taking back my hands.

"You know what? Why don't you just ask Gran Gran about the exact reason she stayed with Grandad when you meet her tomorrow? Huh?" Liberty said flatly, folding her arms.

"It will go so very well, you meeting Gran Gran. Oh yes, like watching a shark try to swim in lava," Lilo snorted, blinking sweetly at me.

That was the moment I wanted to punch Lilo's face off of her face. Punception, I'll call it. Instead, I folded my hands in my lap, in silence, and continued to listen to my family's origin story.

So, after decreeing that Ezekiel would live and extending his and Taresh's life, the Fates stepped back for the next century. They still talked with Ghani, but mostly they let the family experience life without their influence. Unfortunately, the intra-family drama did not go away. Chaos swelled again around the 1930s.

So this is where the family story again gets super fuzzy. It's the part of the timeline that no one wants to talk about, not even Aunt Victoria. Liberty and Leo are unsure of the details, but some major, eternal, life-altering ugliness went down. Whatever occurred, it led to Grandfather Ezekiel disappearing and Mother exiling herself from the family. It's the reason Mother forbade anyone from ever contacting us once we were born. It's the reason she bound our powers and basically had us on the run from our family our whole lives. It's the reason we became the lost branch of the goddess family tree.

Until now.

Now Arden snores on, while sleep eludes me. I stare at the ceiling, questions boomeranging in my mind. What happened to the family in the 1930s? What made Mother turn her back on who she is? What made her hide this gigantic truth from her own daughters decades later? Only my mother could answer those questions for me.

But those aren't the only puzzles in need of solving. The cousins told us most goddesses start displaying their mojo in childhood, around seven or eight years of age. So, not only did Mother lie to us about our entire existences, she suppressed our twin powers for the last decade. When would she finally have said something?

I roll over in my bed and heave a big sigh. I feel like a pinball bouncing between emotional extremes—from hurt to overwhelmed, from dismissive to infuriated—as I sift through my entire life. Before I know it, sunlight begins to creep through the window blinds, sending slices of light across the ceiling, and my anger grows sharp, taking shape as my final response. How could Mother be so selfish, hiding who we are, never giving us a choice in the matter? To bind our powers for ten years so she could continue living the life she wanted? To pretend to be a human family because she chose to abandon her goddess one? We do not deserve to be discovering everything on our like this, only now.

While I can't do anything to resolve my anger with Mother, by the time the sun has fully lit the room, I am resolved in one matter: Arden and I absolutely need to get away from the cousins. I'm done with these emotionally obtrusive, condescending as hell, want-to-be saviors. Lilo is especially the worst. There's no way I can put up with another day in her presence. I mean, really, she's been beyond trying me. I'm surprised the magazines have been the only victims of my irritation. It's taken superhuman strength just to refrain from smacking her—which only proves I'm the one who needs to press the eject button before I self-destruct on the entire group.

Okay, the cousins have done us some major solids: giving us a place to crash tonight; revealing the 411 on our family; showing us how to take control over our mojo. But even though Arden's been smitten with them, I still didn't trust the cousins completely. Like, I accept what they've told us is true, but I don't believe in their motives.

What if the cousins are merely bait sent out to lure Arden and me into a trap? What if this Gran Gran character is actually the Don in the kidnapping scheme to capture Mother *and* us? Despite all the goddess hospitality the cousins have shown us, I'm not convinced it's smart for us to keep following wherever they lead. I feel sick to my stomach at the thought of going to Gran Gran's this morning. I can't just trust everyone and walk further into danger.

I climb down from the top bunk and quietly sneak out the room, taking care not to disturb Arden. Out in the hallway, I tiptoe silently past the cousins' closed bedroom door and continue out to the house phone in the kitchen. When I noticed the phone last night, I thought, *Wow, I have not seen a phone attached to a wall by a cord in ages. What hipster den did they steal it from?* But now I'm beyond grateful it's here, since my cell phone refuses to dial out.

Yesterday, after Arden and I realized our cell phones didn't work, we bought a phone card that would let us call internationally, knowing we'd need to ring up Leo eventually. Now I pull the card out of my pocket and read the code number on it, punching the numbers into the phone. Arden and I had planned to call Leo after we had our cover story down, but I need to *do* something. Now. I can't deal with being inside my own head anymore. I need someone to validate my feelings, my need to escape. Or maybe I just want to hear his voice, a voice of calm in a storm, no matter how angry he is at me.

Leo picks up after just one ring. As soon as I hear a click, I whisper, "Leo? It's Aurora."

"Aurora! You're okay!" I hear his jagged sigh over the crackled line. "Oh my god, are you girls trying to kill me? Where are you? How is Arden? Are you both all right? What are you thinking? What has gotten into you two?"

"Leo, we're all right. I'm sorry, we honestly don't mean to worry you. I hope you got our note, but of course that doesn't make leaving okay. We just really needed to do this. We didn't want to risk you trying to stop us. I understand if you're mad. But we're doing okay. We landed in London safely . . ."

"London! My god, you really flew to London?" Leo shouts from his end of the line.

"Yes." I cringe.

"And where are you in London, exactly?" Leo asks, still yelling.

"Um . . . I think this is the West End? Let me look for an address . . . We connected with our cousins. We're at their place now," I whisper into the phone.

Leo gasps sharply. "Your cousins? Is that what you said?"

There's static, so I move deeper into the kitchen, pulling the phone's spiral cord with me. "Yes, our cousins," I confirm. "Liberty and Leolidessa. They found us at the airport. They want to take us to someone called Gran Gran to help us find Mother."

"Aurora, listen to me," Leo says. "You need to get away from that family out there." His sharp tone slices through the static. I didn't know if Leo had any clue about Mother's real family, until this moment. *How much does he know?*

"Don't . . . if you . . . taken away," the crackling interrupts his words.

"What, Leo?" I press the phone to my ear.

"You can't trust . . . your mother . . . never told you . . ." Leo sounds like he's under a waterfall.

"What are you saying? Leo?"

The static grows and falls, then grows again. Finally, I hear Leo's voice: "You and Arden are so very special. Don't show them who you are." Then I hear a click.

"Hello?" I whisper. "Leo? Are you there?" I wait for more words, heart in my throat, but the only reply is a dead line. "Dammit!" I shout, slamming the phone back to its cradle with more than human force. When I pull my hand away, the phone is cracked down the center.

"Hey! That's a no-no, missy. Always so aggressive!" Lilo says in her singsong voice from just behind me. "Tell our phone you're sorry, princess."

"I'm sorry, phone," I say through gritted teeth, my back to her. Was this obnoxious ball of snot listening to my conversation the whole time?

Lilo must be reading my body language like her favorite magazine because just as I'm imagining the hypersonic punch I owe her, she continues, "Anger might be the source of your power, but you don't have to have it on the ready at all time, Cuz."

*When will this purple pixie stop psychoanalyzing me?* This Lilo chick has been riding me since moment uno! I want at least to verbally annihilate her, just to let off some steam, but I think better of it. Given Leo's final warning, my best plan is to disengage and evacuate as soon as possible. I force myself to take a deep breath before turning around to face her. "I was just trying to connect with our godfather," I tell her. "Arden and I snuck away from him to fly here. He's really worried about Mother and now us."

"Oh, the dude trying to steal my name?" Lilo snorts. "Arden says he's been in love with your mother for forever or something. And he moved to Ohio as soon as you guys settled there? Stalkerazzi, am I right?"

She stands in wait in front of me, wiggling back and forth with her arms crossed. It's like a weirdo road block. Does she think I'm just going to spill some gossip about my mother because she prompted me? I didn't even know when Arden dropped those tidbits on Leo, but I am not going to be the supplier for anything Lilo demands. "Um, yeah, Leo's known Mom since her teens, but they're like brother and sister," I shrug, purposefully unhelpful. "The phone cut out just now. I might try calling him back."

"Ah, that cranky phone is always giving us trouble. We mostly just like how it looks. It's cool right?" Lilo strokes the phone. "Yes, you're very cool. I'm so sorry the mean lady hurt you." She turns and bounces toward me with a sudden grin. "How about we wake up the rest of the girls and get over to Gran's? She always has a huge spread for breakfast, and you can use the phone there!" She links my arm through hers and drags me out the kitchen.

When Lilo turns into the bedroom where she and Liberty spent the night, I quietly shuffle back into the guest room and find Arden still asleep on the top bunk.

"Arden, get up, you," I shake her arm.

After a moment, she mumbles herself awake. "Morning. Are you going to shower first, or should I?" she yawns.

"No. We need to get away from these two chicks, now," I hiss.

"What are you talking about? We love the cousins; why would we leave?" She rubs her eyes, still trying to wake up.

I rest my elbows on her bed, inching closer to her ears. "I know *you* love them, but I don't think they're trustworthy," I whisper. After a pause, I say, "And Leo agrees."

"What? Leo? You spoke with him?" Arden's body straightens with alertness.

"Yes, I called him from the kitchen just now. He's glad we're okay, but when I told him who we're with, he said we need to get away quickly and not to show them who we are. He was serious, Ar."

"But what does he even know?" Arden huffs.

My eyes widen in shock. She'd rather defend fresh-out-the-box cousins over Leo, whom we've known since birth? "Really, Arden! You can't be this naïve. We can't just believe these people because they seem nice. Leo might know the real reason Mother pretends to be an orphan and has never told us about all this 'Caribbean Illuminati with magic' crap. Have you even thought that *they*, the cousins and Gran Gran, might actually be the ones behind the kidnapping?"

"No, they're not. I would sense it." Arden scoots out of the bed and shoos me down the ladder. She descends and starts pulling clothes from her bag to get dressed.

"So, you would sense the danger because of your mental intuition and mind reading? You still can't even use it on me so who's to say they don't have some way of deflecting their true purpose from you right now? What if your powers don't truly exist?" The second I say it, I know it's mean, but I can't help but taunt her about her power deficiency. All night I could use my power against her, easily, but she couldn't get one thought in or out of my head.

Arden sighs as she sits on the side of the bed to put on her tights. There's a long pause before she looks up at me and says, "Is this about my powers or your need to self-destruct? Because they're both very real." When the flare of my nose tells her the burn landed, she continues, "Aurora, I wish you wouldn't keep up this suspicion that everyone around you means you harm—me, the cousins, the entire known universe. Everyone is not conspiring against you to steal your crush or kidnap you for your abilities or whatever you've been dreaming up."

"What?" I sputter in the whiplash back to Devin.

"Look, whatever you or Leo think," Arden says defiantly, "the cousins are family and they love us. They've been waiting half their lives to meet us! And now we are going to meet Gran Gran, who already knows us through her premonitions, and she loves us, too."

Arden pulls on a black skirt over her tights. Dressing up to meet grandmother, always the goody two-shoes. I roll my eyes.

She tries to convince me, "We have to go with them. Gran Gran is going to help us get to Mom. This is the way things have to be, whether you like them or not."

"Girl, this is not a reality-show reunion special; why are you being so obtuse? I can't believe you don't see it! We are walking into a trap—a huge, deadly one." I turn away, force-fully grabbing a shirt and pants from my bag. I throw on the clothes without a thought, focused on getting out of here. Finally, I just say it. "I don't think we should go meet Gran Gran, Arden. There it is. I think we should ditch the cousins on the way and look for Mother alone. That's what we need to do, so let's do it."

"No," she says with more force than I'm used to hearing from her. "Why are you putting up a fight against your very own family? The cousins have told us nothing but the truth, and meeting Gran is the next step in everything we're here for—finding Mom and understanding who we are meant to be. Discovering our family destiny." I hear in her voice that she's already resolved this is the only way, the only path. She sounds like a true convert to the Church of Goddess Scientology.

I groan as I put on my shoes, "Family destiny? You've really chugged the Kool-Aid about this goddess mojo crap? You're just fully on board to follow these chicks wherever they lead? All you need to focus on is that we're freaks, Arden, and we need to get away from these freakier freaks before they freaking kill us."

Arden and I finish dressing in the next moment. As we turn to each other, I gasp with a gross realization that we're twinning way too hard. She's in a red sweater with a giant black heart in the center and black pleated skirt. I threw on a black sweater with a white X in the center, and shiny red jeggings. I usually straighten my hair, but I haven't had time since washing it after the house party, so we each have a lion's mane of dark brown curls framing our faces. It's like we're cosplay for an old school Doublemint gum ad.

"God, I hate being a twin!" I growl and begin taking off my sweater. I feel heat surging through me, but I reach for calm, breathing deeply like Liberty showed me. I don't want my mojo to do something partially regrettable, like accidentally snapping Arden's neck. I close my eyes, trying to reason with my emotions. I'm not truly mad at Arden. I'm just on edge and I don't know what more I can do to convince her that we need to leave. I wiggle out of the red leggings like they've caught on fire.

"You're beyond dramatic, Rora," Arden says. "I can't believe you sometimes! Who cares if we both have red and black on today?" Air puffs out her mouth in frustration. "We're identical twins, okay? Stop hating on it and stop punishing me for being your sister." She stomps off toward the full length mirror in the corner and begins twisting and pinning her hair. "All you want to do is push away anyone who might get close to you, including me. But I can't abandon the chance to rescue Mom from danger just because you don't want to trust the cousins. I just can't. I'm going to meet Gran Gran, with or without you. That's what I need to do."

"Wow!" I freeze in the middle of pulling on my black jeans, my entire body stung. I can barely process what she's said. Through everything in our lives, we have *always*, for better or worse, been together. We're twins, sisters, and as much as we annoy each other, best friends. Of course, I nag her and want to be seen as independent of her, but still . . . we're each other's ride or die, right? Except now, and for these cousins and Gran Gran, Arden is ready to drop me like I'm dead weight? Okay. All right. I see how it is. We can play it that way.

I stand up and start securing all my essentials in my book bag and purse. I can leave where I'm not wanted, make my way to a hotel, and start investigating London on my own. Or maybe I'll just head back home to Ohio, since Arden's got this entire rescuing Mother thing, *without me.*

"Aurora, please stop. I didn't mean it like it came out," Arden says.

I ignore her as I put on my jacket. *With or without you,* she said. Well, "Team Aurora" is ready to proceed without one irritating identical twin.

"I'm sorry," Arden tries again. "I know what I said, but it came out wrong, and it was a rotten thing to say. I don't want us to separate!" I zip up my bag, avoiding her eyes, but I see Arden shake her head hard at me. "Please stay!"

"Oh, don't back down now, sister, it's a 'with or without you' kind of world we live in," I say coolly. "I can't stay with these chicks anymore. It doesn't feel right to me. We can't blindly trust people our mother has avoided for years—and probably for very good reason. I mean, you can, but I just can't. I am out." My hand is on the doorknob and I'm ready to leave without my twin, but Arden swiftly embraces me, and I feel her tears seep down the back of my neck. *Crap.*

"Aurora, I love you, okay? I know it's hard for you to trust and this has been a lot, so I feel you, I really do! I wish you could just hear my thoughts to know for yourself. But it's beyond important that we meet Gran and hear what she has to say. I *feel* it, down to my toes, that she is the only one who can get us started with finding Mom. After that, we can decide if we should go it on our own, but please don't just leave."

"Are you girls about ready to head out to Gran Gran's?" Liberty yells from the hallway.

Arden lets me go, and we hear Lib and Lilo giggling and chatting. I close my eyes, my hand still on the doorknob. I can just *feel* Lilo dancing or doing some other annoying thing on the other side of the door, and I shake my head. They might be dangerous or they might not be, but I can't leave my sister with these kooks. I look at Arden's face as she wipes her tears, and I know my own face is looking pretty defeated. I sigh, hating the decision as I make it. "Okay. We stay together and go to Gran's. But we need to be on guard, because something's not right about all this."

"Okay," Arden nods.

"And I still think we should leave the cousins," I add.

"Totally noted, but we will reassess that particular point after meeting Gran, okay?"

"Okay," I agree. "We both should bring backpacks, in case we need to escape on the fly." Arden starts to protest, but I interrupt, "Okay, just humor me and let me carry your passport."

"Okay," she surrenders, handing me her passport. "Happy now, my sister?"

"No, not at all," I say gruffly, and Arden smiles.

"I know, me neither. Let's go be miserable teenagers who have to meet their grandmother," she says. "Our life is so normal!"

"Oh yeah, we're totally normal." I punctuate the statement by opening the door with my mojo. "Let's go meet the Seer."

AFTER A JOURNEY of two buses and walking five blocks alongside beautifully manicured lawns in front of incredibly thin homes, we arrive at our grandmother's house. It's a remarkably nondescript, khaki-colored, two-level home with a short white gate and an assortment of black garden gnomes guarding a rose bush out front. The porch light is on, even though the morning sun is blazing behind us. Lilo skips ahead of us to ring the doorbell and then hides behind the rest of us once we assemble on the porch. Together we hear footsteps clomping downstairs. The door swings open, revealing an adorable young girl about six years old, with bright hazel eyes and long hair intricately braided with colorful beads. She looks curiously at Arden and me, but her face splits into a wide grin with one look at Liberty.

"It's you!" the girl screeches, and her brown skin begins to glow from the inside, literally beaming brightly, as if her tiny muscles are made of light. I gasp as she rises nearly two feet above her short stature, floating in place as if held up by wires. I glance down to confirm that this girl is levitating in glee. I give Arden a look of surprise. The girl floats back to the ground and she and Liberty embrace warmly, the girl giggling and wiggling inside the hug. I can't help but smile at this baby goddess, effervescent as electric bubbles come to life. "You guys are late!" she cries, wrangling out of the hug. "Gran's been waiting! She's mad. She was even cursing!"

"Really? Thanks for the warning, Mackenzie. Did you make a pound for your swear jar?" Liberty asks.

"I made four!" she says proudly, holding up the digits on one hand.

"I bet you did. Let's get inside then, eh? We've got to show Gran these two, don't we? But anyway, have you grown taller, girly? It's only been a week since we've seen you last. What is Gran feeding you?"

"Only the best food goes in here." She rubs her tiny belly happily. "All the ackee and saltfish and curried chicken and rice and I can eat forever and ever. Come in for breakfast! I helped make the fried dumplings." She tugs on Liberty's arm, and Arden and I follow them into a spacious entryway.

Reggaeton music greets my ears as I look around the room. It has a heavy tropical feel, with warm apricot paint accented by cherrywood stairs and trim. The walls are lined thickly with framed photographs as far as I can see, some in black and white and sepia, others popping with brilliant color. I feel magnetically drawn to them, taking a step closer as I distractedly shrug my coat off my shoulders.

The frames hold images of gorgeous scenes and portraits of people from around the world. In one, three teen girls laugh under a waterfall in a rainforest. While the shot was taken too far away to capture their faces, I'm transfixed by how the waterfall arches unnaturally away from the girls, as if they hold an invisible umbrella. In another photo, a toddler Liberty snuggles her face into the body of a grown lion. The lion's eyes are closed, and I swear the animal is smiling blissfully. I continue down the line until a black and white shot makes me gasp and pause for a closer look. In the frame I see our mother, much younger than she is now and styled like a chocolate Gibson girl, with bouffant hair and intense curves. Tightly held against her hip is a young, sleeping boy, around three or four years old, his face resting in a slightly crooked smile. Mom gazes at him with a look I've never seen on her before, a mixture of pride and surrender. She's completely in love. In most photos with me and Arden, Mom's smile is forced, her eyes distracted. Here, she is glowing, her eyes popped wide open, her cheeks rounded in a huge smile, overflowing with obvious joy. Her hands curve lovingly around his body. Possessively. Motherly. I don't think I've ever felt a bigger urge to punch a picture in my life. Who is this boy from the past that my mother loved so deeply?

"Hey, when was this photo taken?" I ask, still transfixed by the photo. When I turn around, I see no one is paying attention to me or the photographs.

"But Liberty, stop joking! You never come alone!" Mackenzie pushes past Liberty to open the door and look outside. "I know Lilo's here somewhere! Oh, there she is!" The young girl giggles as Lilo, now a black cat with purple streaks, jumps through the door and gracefully leaps into Mackenzie's arms. The girl floats down the hallway and up the stairs with Lilo purring in her grasp. I notice Liberty and Arden taking off their coats and shoes, and I join them. I try to ask about the photo again, but I'm interrupted by a deep, rasping Caribbean voice from inside yelling over a music video blaring from a TV.

"Wagoan, eh? M'ear you, ya know, Lilo and Liberty. Y'll bring't the Yankee twins ere, or ya need more years fi look fi dem?" A husky chuckle emerges, as Gran Gran laughs at her own joke. She knows we're here. She's been expecting us for quite some time. Now she's giving us grief about not getting here quicker. Sass from moment one; it seems certain we're relatives. But Gran Gran's anxiousness for this moment only feeds my dread. I look at the front door, which Liberty is now blocking, as if she knows I might try to leave. So much for a last-minute escape. *I guess this is really happening, this meeting my goddess grandmother thing.* I tug at my wrinkled shirt and shake out my hair with my fingers.

"You look great, Aurora. She's going to love you," Arden nudges me.

"I hate you," I whisper to her as we walk the hallway to the living room.

Liberty follows behind us, poking me in the back when I stall at the doorway. Reluctantly, I enter the room and find myself facing Gran Gran. She's draped along the couch, radiating an aura of confident strength, like a lion at rest. A goddess in all her glory, our grandmother, the Seer, knew we were coming from miles and years away.

She is small yet curvy, and so fit she could bench-press Mackenzie for fun. She has impressively long salt-and-pepper dreads woven into an intricate crown around her head, then spilling along her relaxed length, finally ending on the floor. Her hair is decorated generously with shells, beads, crystals, and other shiny bits. I picture her dragging it from room to room, like a weighty, permanent veil.

For however old she may be, Gran Gran seriously looks *good* for her age. Her face is flawless with smooth, dark brown skin. Her full lips are relaxed in a mysteriously seductive Mona Lisa smile, but it's her eyes that literally take my breath away. Their wide depths change from brown to hazel to green as I gaze into them. I am gobsmacked and intimidated standing in the doorway, wondering if I should bow or curtsey. She winks at me.

"Comyere lilt pickenies, me no bite! De bull you si fi yur eye a cow fi yur heart."

"What did she say?" I whisper back to Liberty.

"Gran Gran speaks like a true Jamaican, in Patois and quick fables. She says don't be afraid of her; she's a softie in disguise."

I gulp. *Yeah, right.* Arden's hand sneaks its way into mine. I'm not sure if it's to soothe her or me, but I'm grateful for something to hold onto.

"Gran, this is Aurora and Arden, Selene's twins from America," Liberty announces us from across the room. "You gotta talk clean around them—they never hear Patois."

Gran Gran smiles. She knows we have no idea what she's saying, she's just messing with us. Okay, then. I know what to do when there's another wise-ass in the room. Be bold and direct. I take a breath and move closer, to the heart of the room. "Hello, Gran Gran," I say.

Arden echoes me. "It's great to finally meet you, Gran Gran. We've heard a lot about you from Lib and Lilo."

"Ah, they been mouths-a-massie for you? But me sure you heard nothing pon me from your mama. And look how she still living so far from her kitchen; you Yankee girls so skinny! Like these video girls, eh? I don't know what they think they have to shake! Come sit down, you two need to eat, now! Mackenzie?" she calls loudly.

After a moment, the girl appears in the doorway with Lilo, still in cat form, now dressed in doll clothes, wrapped in her arms. "Yes Grandmama?" she asks, her head bouncing side to side.

"Baby girl, start making these tiny Yankees a plate of breakfast before they waste away. And Lilo hates when you dress her up. Leave that girl alone so she can say hello."

Mackenzie pouts for a moment, then sets Lilo down before floating off to the kitchen. We all burst out laughing when we see Lilo's full outfit—a pink frilly dress, bonnet, and slippers. Lilo crosses the room, clearly vexed, kicking and hissing angrily. She was playing nice for Mackenzie before, but now she tries her best to wiggle the bonnet off. Unfortunately, she's trapped. We continue chuckling as Liberty bends down to undress her.

Finally free, Lilo shifts back into human form. "Ugh, so much better! That girl wants a cat so badly, but she's not allowed until I approve of her treatment and, psh, from to-day's assessment, she's nowhere near getting one! She wouldn't even let me breathe!" Lilo leaps and twirls gracefully across the room to Gran, then bows to kiss her on the cheek.

"My precious Lilo. Kensie will have her cat soon, but yes, she needs training from her sweet cousin." She chuckles and adds, "What a man doan know older dan him."

I raise my eyebrow at Liberty, and she whispers the translation, "Everyone needs experience."

Gran Gran lifts the remote beside her and turns off the TV, then slowly rises from the couch. With one hand, she wraps and drapes the length of her hair over an arm, holding it like an escort to a dance. She nods towards the dining room table, and Liberty pinches my arm to get me moving into a seat. The four of us sit as Gran Gran glides over, the ends of her dreads trailing behind her like a train. Once she sits at the head of the table, she snaps her fingers and Mackenzie floats into the room, followed by four levitating plates piled with ackee and saltfish, cooked bananas, fried dumplings, and four cups filled with steaming liquid.

"Tank you, me love," she says, kissing Mackenzie on the cheek. The plates and cups land softly in front of Arden, me, and the cousins.

"You're welcome Gran Gran. Enjoy everyone!" Mackenzie floats up the stairs to finish a special project she promises to share with us before we leave.

After Gran says grace in thick Patois, there is an extended silence; we are all too busy stuffing our faces to make conversation. The food is so delicious that if the house caught on fire, I wouldn't hesitate to bring the plate along with me. The spiciness of the ackee, the saltiness of the fish, the sweetness of the banana cooked in butter and salt while still green, and the buttery crunch of the dumplings all compete for best flavor in my mouth. I take a sip of the hot chocolate tea, yes, chocolate tea, and I am so in love with the pure cocoa flavor that I moan in delight as its warmth fills my belly. If this is eating like a Jamaican goddess, I am totally all in.

"So, Yankees, tell me about yourselves." Gran says from the head of the table, with Arden and I seated to each side of her.

My mouth is full, and while I chew I wonder what kind of Seer needs telling anything? Doesn't she just know everything about me already? I'm a true skeptic, and I'm sure my vibes will kill the mood, so I say nothing.

After a few beats, Arden takes the lead. "Well, we grew up travelling on tour with Mom, bouncing between cities and countries around the world for most of our lives. Mom got a teaching gig at the University of Cincinnati for a semester just last year. When it was wrapping up, Aurora insisted we all stay so that she and I could finish high school in one place. So we stayed."

I cough from surprise, unconsciously interrupting Arden. Is she trying to pin us being in Cincinnati completely on me? It may have started as my fight, but it was Arden who gave Mother the final push to make us stay. Being in Ohio has benefitted all three of us. She glances at me now, and I squint my eyes at her before she continues on to Gran Gran.

"So yeah. We're now finishing our senior year in high school in Ohio. It's in the Midwest of America."

"Oh yeah? Midwest?" Gran Gran chuckles to herself. "And you like that, living in the corn fields like a quashie?"

At Gran Gran's question, Lilo snorts into her chocolate tea.

"Yes," Arden says, no hesitation. "I mean, it is what it is. It's less city than London, for sure, but it's no farm town either. People are really connected to their families, their friends, even as a stranger you feel embraced by it. The city has this quiet hum that touches everything. I like it." She smiles brightly, and I am amazed at the light in my sister's eyes. Does she really love living in Cincinnati this much? How did I not know this about her? I look at Gran Gran, whose eyes are now a deeply bright violet.

"Me like you, Yankee girl. You know dat every ho hav dem 'tick a bush," Granny says, and now I'm the one to snort in my chocolate tea.

"Don't choke, Cuz. She's just saying that there's a place for everyone," Liberty chuckles next to me.

"Yes, Miss Aurora don't let Arden steal your tongue," Gran Gran says to me, her eyes melting to a light brown as they hold mine hostage. "How do you feel about Ohio?" she asks softly.

I pause, deciding between being completely honest and politely vague. "Well, it's the first place I feel like I've really lived a life that was mine." I shrug as honesty wins and the words tumble out of my mouth. "We've been all around the world, but in Cincinnati I can finally be myself and have my own life that isn't just about being Mom's daughter or Arden's twin sister. So, I like it there."

"Okay, I see." Gran Gran closes her eyes as she speaks. "You like the sense of freedom while having the safety of staying inside a bubble, eh?"

I nod, then I realize she can't see me with her eyes closed. But she continues as if she did.

"But the people . . . how do you feel about *them*?" she presses, leaning forward, her eyes now open, glowing amber as they read my face.

"I . . . they're . . ." I stop myself, realizing I have nothing profound to say about the people of Ohio. They're normal? Soft? Easily impressed? The friends I've made in the past year have run as deep as a bird bath. They're great as an entourage, but I don't feel, like, connected to any one of them. Should I? I'm suddenly embarrassed. I've failed a test for lack of studying. "The people are okay," I respond into my nearly empty plate.

Gran cocks her head to the side, "What is this *okay*?" Her mouth twists in a wry grin as she repeats the word, "Okay," like it's unknown to her.

"They're just . . . not . . . I just don't know how I feel about the people, all right?" I say, turning my head away, wanting this line of questioning ended.

Gran Gran pulls my chin, turning my head back to her with a smile, like I've said something cute. Her eyes shift to a lilac gray as she stares into mine. "That is your first lie in this house," she declares, raising an eyebrow, waiting for me to deny it. "You know how you feel, Madame Lashy, no baca play bro Annanci pon mi. Eh?" Even without Lib's translation, I understand Gran knows I'm whitewashing myself. We squint at each other, an impromptu staring game.

I crack first and decide to give her me, no lies. "I think the people are boring and predictable, and I don't really care about them."

Arden gasps, "Aurora, that's horrible!"

But Gran Gran just continues smiling at me, and I'm encouraged to expand. "But it's fun being popular and having people look to me. I'm enjoying that."

"Enjoying what exactly, eh?" Gran asks softly.

"Being needed." That answer came from a true and deep place inside. "I want to feel like I matter to people. Most of the time I don't." I look to Arden, and her face is pained.

"I need you. Mom needs you," she pleads, and I shake my head, totally over that fallacy.

"We're in this mess because the one thing Mother

needs most is to be on stage," I tell her. "And you? You're either in your own head or trying to press your agenda on me. Like confronting me the day Mom left, instead of just giving me space till I was ready to talk. It's all about you, and somehow you're surprised I don't feel like I really matter?"

"Ultra-ouch, Cuz," says Lilo from her seat next to Arden. "You shouldn't burn your sister like that."

"Yeah, Aurora, you must know how much your sister loves you," Liberty adds.

I twitch. "I do know that she has the ability to speak for herself. Do you two know that?" The words come out with grit, and I feel intoxicated with anger. I imagine throwing the cousins through the window with my mojo, and I wonder if they'll keep pushing till it happens.

Lilo, of course, steamrolls on like her sole purpose in life is to press my buttons. "Cuz, I understand you're upset, but we have a right to defend Arden if you're being unfair."

"A right? I'm still trying to figure out who you two even are in my life, and you're talking about rights?" I rise, ready to leave this crew for the second time today. I might have been in my own blind spot before, but the words that tumbled out to Gran were the truth. I don't feel needed. This realization catapults me into movement. I don't need people who don't need me, and I am done here. "Look, Gran Gran, this breakfast was delicious and all, but—" I wipe my mouth with a napkin and move away from the table.

"No, don't go Rora!" Arden stands, too, and the cousins also rise to action.

"Everyone will stay seated until I say they are excused!" Gran Gran commands loudly, her eyes black with specks of gold. Power radiates from her body in warm waves, though she remains calmly seated. The room trembles at her words; the table shakes under my hands; the lights flicker. Arden, the cousins, and I get our butts back in our seats. Gran is not to be effed with.

I smile meekly and offer a blanket apology to our scarily powerful grandmother goddess. "Sorry. Sometimes I get heated." My mouth twitches at the understatement, and Gran's eyes soften to dark gray.

"You *should* be sorry, for what you said," sasses Lilo from across the table.

"But," Gran interrupts with a click of her tongue, "she is right. You need to stay out of their quarrel, Lilo and Liberty. Cat no business inna fowl fight."

Lilo's face drops, and I can't help but stick my tongue out at her while Gran isn't looking my way.

"And you wanna lose that sharp tongue today, I see," Gran says, turning back to me.

"How did you . . ." I begin to ask, then stop.

"You think Gran can only see with the eyes on her face, huh?" she chuckles. "Arden, tell me all about your new boyfriend."

Arden's cheeks flush, and she bites her lip. "I don't have a boyfriend . . . I've never had a boyfriend."

Gran grabs Arden's hand from the table and squeezes it, smiling as her eyes melt into a deep violet. "Aaahh, such an old soul you are, my quiet storm. You've already met the first of many loves of your life."

Arden's eyes nearly pop out of her head. "Devin?" she whispers.

Gran smiles and nods slightly.

"I only just met him." Arden glances at me for a moment. "It was intense. I saw visions of us together. He said he's been dreaming of me. I don't understand any of it. What does it mean? Who is he?"

"Your heart is ready for love, so it has called to him," Gran says. "He is who you are meant to be with now, so he was summoned." She chuckles at Arden's raised eyebrows. "It's a special thing the Fates gave your mother, and it appears you have it as well. You have a heart for loving deeply, and it searches and finds true love then calls it forward." Gran squeezes Arden's hand. "The men whom you are destined to love will be summoned by you. They will come. Just enjoy falling in love and know it is meant to be, my sweet granddaughter."

"What?" Arden shakes her head. "But I don't understand. I didn't suddenly decide I wanted a boyfriend. I don't even know this guy. Why him? Why me?"

"Did you not hear me, child?" Gran laughs warmly, a robust sound that reflexively brings a smile to my face. "There's nothing to understand. Your heart is ready. It is. Done! He is the proof. Your head, ugh, it's too full of emotions to decide anything, eh? The heart of a goddess always knows when it's ready for, or done with, a man." Gran Gran continues chuckling, "Look at you! Frustrated, confused. You think you can understand everything? No, you cannot. But you *feel* I am right? Your heart so transparent, your head so cloudy! So much like Selene!" When saying Mother's name Gran Gran's eyes shift to an aqua blue. "Selene eventually decided to go with her heart, you know. In matters of love, in matters of life. She leads with her heart, that girl," she sighs, "which sometimes means she doesn't make the smartest moves. But you will, quiet storm." Gran closes her eyes and reinforces her grip on Arden's hand.

"You live so deep inside yourself," she continues. "But you're on the path to living out loud. It frightens and excites you. This is good. Lean into it. You're coming into your own. You feel intensely, but I see you very full of light and love. You're one of the brightest of us all, in so many ways. You can hear and see and touch what others cannot, right through the mind, to the heart." Gran sighs and shudders slightly, as if she sees something troubling, "You carry your worries deeply. Whe di goat do, di kid wi falla. So very much like your mother, you a worrier and protector."

I manage to keep my snort of disbelief to myself this time. Is she referring to the lady who abandoned us? Who has lied to us our entire lives? Because that lady isn't worried about anyone but herself. Doesn't Gran Gran realize Mother is constantly thirsting for attention? A woman who needs to chase adoration from strangers around the globe isn't protecting anything but her inflated ego. I shake off the anger and tune back into Gran's reading of Arden.

"Do you know where our mother is?" Arden asks.

"No, granddaughter, I'm sorry. I don't know where she is. But I know it is up to you and your sister to save her. It is your quest to find her. The Fates have even locked me in place to prevent me from searching, but I know she's still alive. I know it." Gran Gran caresses Arden's cheek. "You and your mother are very close, I see. I know. You two are still connected, even now. Can't you feel her?"

Arden nods in reply, exhaling a hard breath.

"She's been reaching out to you, waiting for you, eh?" Gran sighs. "She's growing faint. But she is holding on. You need to find her soon."

"But is she even still in London? How do we find her?" Ar asks, leaning into our Grandmother. I lean in, too, as the answer comes.

"She's still in London, being hidden somewhere. You're the key to uncovering her location, quiet storm," she says to Arden.

I blink hard, stung at my apparent uselessness.

Gran continues, "It's your power. Your strong connection. Hag wash inna di fuss water him ketch. I can tell you the next step on the path, and the remaining are yours. You must go to your cousin Kiara now. Liberty will take you to her. She lives in the south of the city. If you join together with her powers, you should be able to locate Selene's mind and rescue her before it's too late."

I see the worry in Arden's furrowed brow, and Gran must as well. She cups Arden's face, her eyes a violet sea as she says, "You can do this. Be smart and cunning and swift. You know you're a goddess now, right? Shine your light through the dark and find your mother."

They smile at each other, and it's as if they are inside their own bubble. So, Teacher's Pet Arden has made another conquest, first the cousins and then Gran Gran. I'm not even sure why I'm here, since Arden's the only one anyone really wants. I clear my throat loudly and Gran finally looks to me.

"And you, my fire starter. Give me ya 'and. I know you tink me na right and off me rockas, but let me give ya some knowledge to clear that head full of anger you carry around. Di olda di moon, di brighter it shine."

She grabs my hands and her eyes grow, switching from dark blue to a murky green, like a swamp. I wiggle like a two-year-old being dragged to the naughty corner. I know Gran won't be letting me go till I've heard all she has to say, but I don't want to hear it. The truth is, I'm scared. I don't want her reading me. I don't want her to truly see me. There's something dark inside me. Something that makes me undeserving of love and definitely unworthy of my goddess status. I just know Gran Gran's going to see it. She jerks my arm and tightens her grip on my hand. Suddenly I can't move at all.

"Such a fighter you!" she chuckles with a wink at me, her eyes a swirl of green, gold, red, and grey. *Are those the colors she is seeing inside my soul?* "You no fallow-fashion at all, missy, eh? You say, you do what you want. You're rebellious, my Yankee goddess. Hmph . . . yes you are! Me like you, for true. But inside . . . hmm, look at it! It's so much!" Gran closes her eyes and I feel her thumb pressing across my skin like she's reading Braille.

"So confused as to who your motivations make you. So afraid of what is deep inside. Gran can see you girl, you're no villain! De bess a field mus' have weed." She clucks her tongue and stares me down with soft grey eyes. "You really hate being hurt, being disappointed. You're afraid everyone will abandon you. So you push them away first, right? You're like a marshmallow hiding behind a wall of fire! Be true to yourself, softie. Drop the defenses and show us who you are!" Gran Grans eyes blaze amber gold.

I grunt, rejecting her assessment. I am not *soft*! I do not push people away! "Do you know who has Mother?" I ask directly, stepping aside my frustration.

Gran's eyes shift through so many colors—indigo with yellow, hazel green with flashes of orange. They finally settle to a dark blue like the depths of the ocean before she speaks, dropping the Patois as she says, "That's not the real question you want to ask me, eh? You want to know why I spared my husband's life so long ago. I'll answer both together. There has, for so long, been a war within our family. It was started because of a blessing that the Fates and the Celestial Beings gave to me and to my daughters. But you must understand, there's always a curse along with any blessing. And the stronger the blessings, the stronger the curse.

"While the women of this family grew more powerful, your grandfather, too, became different—darker, corrupted by envy and greed. The parts of himself that were once loving and vulnerable were eaten away to nothing. I tried my best to save him, to love him back to himself, but evil grows and infests the heart, seeping into every corner like black mold. There's nothing to slow its growth once it has taken hold. My husband was particularly jealous of Selene as she became the most talented goddess of our family."

I snort, and Gran's eyes turn an acid green like a sour apple.

"The lack of respect that you continue to display toward your mother is highly unbecoming of a goddess in training. I know you have experiences that lead you to think you know her, but I know who my daughter is. You will listen with an open mind and respect that I have insight that will help you and Arden save her."

I gulp, my face boiling from the telling off, and nod. I am sure Lilo is gloating, but I don't dare turn away from Gran's green eyes.

After a beat, her eyes fade back to gray. She nods, satisfied I've received the message, and continues her story. "Selene's first child was a boy. She named him Zion. He was bright and strong and so handsome." Gran's voice catches and she clears her throat.

I look to Arden—shit is getting real. We had a brother we never knew about? This must be the little boy in the photo.

"Zion was about fifteen when he started displaying some talents of his own; the first of any man in our family. Zion was always strong, but he became superhuman overnight. He was always charming, but suddenly girls were literally threatening suicide if he didn't love them back. It was the early 1920s in England, and everyone noticed a young black man with that much magnetism. Not at all in a positive way."

Her eyes grow dark gray and I feel the table tremble slightly. "What happened to Zion?" I whisper.

Flashes of red swirl into her eyes, and anger enters her voice for the first time. "A man accused Zion of attacking his daughter and confronted him in the street. Zion tried to reason, but the man only wanted blood. When Zion fought him off easily, dozens of men jumped into the fray, attacking him with everything they had. He had superhuman strength, but he couldn't take an entire mob by himself. It was a savage and brutal beating. He barely made it home before he died in Selene's arms." Gran brushes a tear from her eye. "We raged and mourned for weeks. Selene was . . . there is no way to describe a mother at the death of her first and only child. My husband went missing at this time, and we assumed he was searching for answers or enacting revenge for Zion. Months passed, but still he never returned, so we started hunting for him, fearing that he had also met a violent end." She sighs shakily and closes her eyes. "We eventually discovered that my husband, Selene's father, had helped spread the hateful lie that brought the end to Zion's life."

My jaw drops, and I hear Arden gasp.

"It was the worst time in any lifetime I have lived," Gran says. "To lose my grandson and watch my daughter spiral into madness, all while knowing the evil scheme was brought together by a jealous man I had loved for centuries. Selene nearly died from heartbreak, and her powers faded from her one by one."

I pictured our flighty, ever-joyous Mother wailing and pulling out her hair in grief, left with the horror of the murder and betrayal of the two most important men in her life. I always thought of her as pampered, spoiled, never experiencing anything more traumatic than the loss of a favorite pair of shoes. I swallow, trying to soothe my suddenly dry mouth. I really, really don't know Mother. Not at all.

"Over a decade passed and we never did find any trace of my husband. Selene barely ate or slept for years, and she eventually lost the ability to speak. The weight of her grief was unbearable, but she refused to let anyone shoulder it with her. She worried about us. She wanted to protect us."

Gran pauses, raising an eyebrow at me, and I gulp, nodding at her. "To communicate she would write letters, wonderful poetry about her day or observations about people. She could be a writer, your mother."

Gran winks at Arden, and I watch my twin beam with pride. It's her life passion to be a writer, and it's now confirmed that those skills actually come from Mother. Great, yet another thing they have in common that they don't need me for. *I'm just collecting Ls today*, I think, but Gran snaps her fingers at my face.

"Focus. You've barely begun and have far to go, my rebel Yankee girl. So, for years after she lost everything, even her voice, your mother could only write letters. I kept them, they were beautiful and hopeful, so we all thought maybe she would come back to us . . . but then we all got the final letter, the goodbye letter. It said Selene was leaving us, leaving the family, leaving London and Jamaica as home forever. She would find a new path for her life. It said she no longer considered herself a goddess, and, even if she gained any gifts back, she would never return to the family or speak of her past to anyone. She said after Zion, she couldn't imagine having children ever again, but if she did, we were never, ever to seek them out in any way. She didn't want you open to the dangers your gifts could bring." Gran Gran closes her eyes like she is reviewing a memory from her mind. "But I knew I would see you both. I saw it. The day you two were born, I had the strongest vision of my life that I would meet my powerful twin granddaughters the day when they needed me the most, to rescue Selene from her father."

My head is spinning from all Gran's told us, and I nearly

choke at how casually she drops the answer to my question. "Wait, you know he's the one who has Mother? Her own father is trying to kill her, again? Why would he do this?" The table starts quaking, the dishes and glasses rising and spinning in midair, food and drinks flying to the walls. It's my rage, I realize, but I can't access the new breathing techniques to control myself.

Gran Gran's eyes widen, red-orange, molten lava, but she stays perfectly still.

The cousins and Arden jump away screaming, but I can barely hear them. I'm overwhelmed by a fevered desire to rip Ezekiel apart. He's the source of every trauma in my life right now, and I'm beyond playing nice. The doors of the china cabinet across from us fly open, the dishes flinging themselves wildly around the room. Arden and the girls duck underneath the table, pulling the tablecloth down to protect them from the shards.

"Stop this, Aurora," Gran Gran whispers to me, her eyes swirling crimson.

"I can't," I whisper back through gritted teeth, my whole body shaking with anger.

Gran's eyes tighten, darkening near black as another dish crashes against the wall. She flips my hand on the table, palm upward, and slaps her own into mine. In a flash, the room blackens around me.

"AURORA. AURORA?"

I feel someone pinching my arm. I'm startled awake, drool dripping down my chin. "What the hell?!" I sputter, finding the room put back together and the cousins and Arden seated exactly where they had been, each of them looking to me with worry.

"Precisely," Gran Gran says. "Did you think you could come into my home, my domain, and act however you want? Throwing the type of toddler goddess tantrum that even Mackenzie has grown out of? I can control every single thing in this house. Everything. Including your powers, from the moment you stepped in the door."

My jaw drops, and Gran cocks her head at me, her eyes now a deep lavender.

"But I shouldn't need to control your powers, you see. You should be able to. I know it's new to you, eh, but you're capable." She looks at me closely for a moment then chuckles. "Okay, I see now. You just *choose* to be wild, huh? You think that's your way, the only way you can be?"

I stay silent, breathing slowly, conscious of my cold palm still connected with Gran Gran's. She wraps her fingers around my hand, squeezes it, and warmth and energy flood my body.

"Let me tell you a story about someone else who chose to stay wild, huh? Brer Anansi was wild. He was a smart and cunning spider. Every one of his animal friends knew never to bet against him because he always found a clever way to win, no matter what. In truth, Brer Anansi didn't really care who he hurt. He remained wild, even when he married a beautiful female spider named Crooky and even when he had his own son."

I look to the others, wondering why Gran Gran is suddenly telling us some children's story about a spider. But

I've learned my lesson about interrupting and stay quiet as she continues.

"Years passed and the land went into a drought. Food was scarce. When Brer Anansi went searching for food he found only two plantains to bring home for himself and his family. His friends said, 'Okay, you are a husband and a father, the land is in drought, you must abandon your self-centered ways, finally. You must give one plantain to your wife and one to your son.'

"But Brer Anansi was more cunning than they even knew. He went home and cooked the plantains up nice. He set three plates at the table, but only plated out the two plantains in front of his wife and son. As the family bowed their head for grace, Brer Anansi thanked the heavens for his wife, thanked them for his son, begged for forgiveness for his selfish, wild ways, prayed for the end of the drought, pleaded on behalf of his belly, and finally asked that he make it through the night without starving to death, as he knew the best thing he could do was to go hungry in the face of his wife and son's hunger. Both Crooky and her son were weeping heavy tears at the prayer by Brer Ananci. Neither hesitated in cutting their own plantain in half and loading a piece onto Brer Ananci's empty plate.

"And that's how even at the height of a drought, Brer Ananci was cunning enough to eat even better than his own wife and son, and how his friends finally learned they should never bet against him winning in the end."

Gran Gran's eyes, once a dark olive tone, now swirl with an electric green. "Ezekiel. Your grandfather. I don't know how many times he used to tell the children that story. He loves that story. He is that story. A selfish, wild man, determined to use and manipulate whatever, whomever, to keep himself winning. He's cunning. He uses people and what they love to achieve his aim. It's those closest to him that are in the most danger of being used in the worst ways. Don't you see what he's doing?" Gran Gran's eyes flash between green and orange.

I swallow hard and shake my head no.

"He's using Selene to get to you two. I don't know why." She sighs. "But I know him, and I know there's more to this than killing your mother. Although he won't hesitate to do that if it doesn't look like he's going to get what he wants."

"So, let me get this straight," I say, tucking my hair behind my ear. "It's a trap. We're all aware it's a trap. But you're sending us into it anyway?"

"Because otherwise your mother dies."

"This is just . . ." The table begins shaking again, and Gran Gran squints her eyes at me. I take a breath, forcing myself to stay calm. "Why can't you save her yourself? Or get the Fates to fix this mess? Aren't you supposed to be powerful enough for that?"

"Rora!" Arden says, slapping the table.

"No, she's right," Gran Gran says. "I, too, am frustrated that I can't do more. I pled to save his life so long ago, and the Fates said it was the last time they would intervene in such a way. They know they had a hand in creating the monster that Ezekiel is today, but they won't step in further. We have to solve this within the family. My only role in this was to wait till you came to me and to tell you all I know. It's up to you now. I know that Ezekiel lured your mother here under threat to you two. I don't know why he's waited till now, or what his bigger plan might be, but I know for certain he is the one who has kidnapped her. It is now up to you both to decide what you want to do with this truth. I hope that you will use it to save Selene."

*Man, she's good*, I admit with a sigh. Gran is right. My anger at Mother has no roots, given the light of the complete truth. In fact, I don't truly know my own mother. I never did. She was never here for the opera, but to protect us from a psychotic and murderous grandfather. She has loved and lost more than I could ever have imagined. She must love Arden and me more than I ever gave her credit for, to gladly give herself up to the one person she hates more than anything. This realization twists my stomach in knots, and I feel more villainous than ever. *What is wrong with me?*

"We're going to save her, Gran Gran," Arden says. "We'll leave right now for Kiara's." Arden and the cousins rise. I start moving, too, and Gran squeezes my hand one final time.

"Aurora, your sister and your mother need you, just the way you are, always," Gran Gran says softly.

I avoid her eyes because inside me, I feel the exact opposite of her words are true. I have been rotting from the inside out. I've been hating myself, hating others and holding onto expectations no one can fulfill. Now all I have is unjustified anger and emptiness. Gran thinks they need me, but I can't be there for Arden or Mother.

I think of Arden's words earlier today, and even though she took them back, I now believe them: she and Mother would be better off without me. I don't have anything good to give either of them. I've been so pissed at both of them this whole time, not even giving Mother an ounce of credit or mercy. I'm not what they need, and I don't want to spoil their lives with my rotten core. Mother deserves so much better. I'm absolutely horrible. She probably won't even want to look at me when she hears how I've been acting since she left us in Ohio. Wild. Self-centered. We're so alike, I bet Grandfather Ezekiel threw wild house parties, too.

We are making our goodbyes to Gran when Mackenzie reappears with her laptop, demanding we stay for just two more seconds. She has crafted a video dedicated to her love of Lilo as her cat. The hilariously adorable video features photos of Lilo in horrible costumes, hugged up by Mackenzie, who sings a voice-over chorus.

"Lilo's my cat/slim and not fat/dressed like a rat/Lilo's all that."

Gran, the cousins, and Arden are in hysterics while Mackenzie floats happily around the room hugging everyone, including me. All I can do is smile wanly. I need to get away from all these good, loving people before I ruin them.

We open the door, and I am surprised that it's nearly dusk.

"It didn't feel like we spent all day in there . . . but apparently we did?" I say to Lilo and Liberty as we walk to the bus stop to catch the first of many transfers to South London.

"Oh yeah. So . . . coming to see Gran always takes longer than it feels like it does. It takes a while for her to commune with the Fates, but she's able to fold time while she's awaiting the message, so it doesn't feel as long as it takes to get a reading from her. That's why she decided to move to London decades ago. She finds it easier to fold time here."

I'm really not sure I understand this, but I find myself lacking enough care to ask any follow up questions. I'm hungry and irritated and jet-lagged, and I don't know who my own mother is, and my sister deserves to be a goddess, but I clearly don't, because I'm pretty sure I'm the evil twin. We arrive at the bus stop, weeds growing up through cracks in the sidewalk. I begin picking at my cuticles while Liberty tells us all she knows about Kiara.

"Kiara's really beautiful and super brilliant. She's Mackenzie's older sister. Their mother is our Aunt Victoria in Jamaica. She sent her girls here to go to school and learn from Gran," Liberty says, but I can tell there is more to the story.

"So why doesn't Kiara just live with Gran and Mackenzie here?" Arden asks, and I nod in agreement; if she lived here now, we wouldn't have to wait on the bus.

"Um, so I would never call anyone in our family weird. Let's just say Kiara's eccentric, or at least her powers are," Liberty says with careful tact.

"It's only since Mackenzie was born, her powers just got . . ." Lilo closes her mouth at Liberty's look.

"Oh yeah, the exponential sister power thing," Arden says.

"Yeah. Kiara was fifteen when Mackenzie was born. As a teen, her powers were still developing, you know, and then Mackenzie . . . well, you saw her, she's a goddess prodigy and she has so many abilities and such control at six years old! So anyway, when she was born, Kiara's main talent got, well, kinda out of hand, let's say. Yeah. Out of hand. That's a good way to put it."

Continuing to pick at my cuticles, I rip back the skin and watch blood seep around my thumb. I look up at Liberty, "What do you mean out of hand? I don't get why she can't live with Gran and her own sister." I have a really bad feeling about this new relative we have been sent to meet.

"So, okay, don't freak out, Cuz, but it's like she lives on multiple physical planes at once and can travel instantly through space. Also, sometimes she emits low level radioactive charges that she can't help, and it turns out that with extended exposure she can be damaging to developing children, well, developing goddess children. I'm more than positive she's okay around mortal kids. It was just no bueno with all the powers growing and mixing and spiking. Anyway, that's why she lives apart from Mackenzie and Gran in the south."

"What the absolute hell?!" I yelp. "She's radioactive?! Why are we going to hang out with her?"

"Because she's the next step in finding Mom, remember?" Arden pokes my arm, and I slap her hand away.

"And how do you know Kiara will even be home?" I continue with a grunt. "How does someone who accidentally space travels live in South London?" I stomp on a dandelion, angry that no one is appropriately reacting to the madness of this situation but me.

"Kiara astronomically projects herself from one plane to the next," Liberty says, making shapes with her hands. "There's something about the place in South London though. It's like it's on a fault line or something. Anyway, at least one of her selves is always at home. Gran said she'll call her to tell her we're on the way."

Liberty's words do nothing to my ease my anxiety and irritation.

"It's going to be okay, Rora. We're going to get to Mom. We just have to keep following this yellow brick road," Arden says.

I shake my head, rejecting her forced brightness. I pull her arm, leading her to the far side of the bus stop, away from the cousins. "It's literally impossible for this family to get any more bizarre or more dangerous. Seriously! Ar, can we please just leave them now?" I'm shaking with poorly controlled anxiety.

"Are you serious? We can't leave now! They know how to get to Aunt Kiara, and she's the next step to getting to Mom. You heard Gran Gran—this is our mission!" Arden looks at my fingers. "Are you bleeding? Rora! Are you picking at your cuticles again?!"

"Just shut up about that!" I scream, stuffing my hands in my pockets. Lilo dances over to us and I have to squeeze my hands to my sides to keep from shoving her away.

"Is everything alright twinsies? I know things got pretty major back there. Apparently, you had a big brother! Let's discuss, how do we feel about that?"

"Lilo, can you please just let my sister and me talk for a minute? That'd be, like, so super great if you could back off for once, pretty please?"

"Extra sharp cheddar cheese, can my sis and I talk, pretty please?" Lilo sings while dancing away.

Involuntarily I roll my eyes, then I take a deep breath before turning back to Arden. "Look, do you really believe a radioactive schizophrenic is going to help us win back Mother? Arden, this is bat shit bananas. Every bit of it. We need to leave, and right now."

"No, honestly, it's going to work, Rora! I'll just need to learn some of Kiara's space travel power and combine it with my mental connection to Mom and locate her mind. Then we can go save her from our evil granddad."

"Wow, okay, yeah, you've got it all planned out. Can you even hear yourself? Can you hear me? It's like you don't even need me," I say flatly.

"Of course, I need you!" Arden opens her mouth to say more, but she's drowned out by the cousins behind us.

"Oh no, Lilo, your xerox machine is coming this way!" Liberty screeches.

"Goddess alive, why does Fanny always find me no matter where I am?" Lilo throws her hands in the air. "It's like she can smell how much I hate her! I hate her so much it's like a full-time job. It completes me."

"I hate her so much I've been trying to develop the ability to make people disappear, just so I can use my powers exclusively on her," Liberty says.

"I hate her so much that I once had a dream I pulled out her fingernails with pliers. But then I woke up . . . and I hated her even more for making me torture her in my subconscious," Lilo counters.

"Damn, Lilo. That one went dark," Liberty chides. They both laugh.

"Who are you talking shit about so hard?" I ask.

Liberty gestures to two girls walking our way. "The one in the pink. Her name is Tiffany, but she's always up under Lilo's butt, so we just call her Fanny."

"What do you mean?"

"She's a serial copycat. If Lilo has a cold, Fanny'll go get influenza and say she invented being sick," Liberty says as a matter of fact. "But beyond that, she's rude, manipulative, and so jealous of Lilo and me it verges on obsession."

"She snogged my last girlfriend just to eff up our rela- tionship!" Lilo snorts. "Not that I care or even remember that that happened."

"But why are you guys hating on her?" I question. "Maybe she just liked her, too."

Lib and Lilo look at me like I've grown a tree out the side of my neck.

"No, Cousin. No," Liberty says, shaking her head.

"Listen, if there was a reality show for the most hating hater ever, they could save money on production and cast- ing and just give her the grand prize. Because that bitch is a hay-ter." Lilo's eyes are on Fanny's hot pink clubbing outfit. "At least they'll be taking a different bus than we are for the clubs . . . and, I wore that exact dress in black three weeks ago. She knows she knows."

"She totally knows," Liberty says, clicking her tongue. "She looks horrible in it."

I turn away from Lilo and Lib's hatefest to take in Fanny—no, Tiffany—and her friend as they near our cor- ner. Both girls are hot and super done up. High heels, skintight dresses, makeup and hair—a night on the town is going down, and I find myself in my own hatefest. Today has made me feel so old, but I want so badly to feel almost eighteen again. I want to go dancing. I want to kiss a cute boy. I want the stress of truth and reality to give way to pounding music and pulsing bass. I want to join them and forget about this family of liars and protectors and murderers and goddesses I have been told is mine.

Since this morning, I have felt nothing but horrible. Yes, I'm ashamed that I judged Mother wrongly, but I'm still enraged that she never told us any of this, that she bound our powers for years, that she let me believe lies about her instead of telling me the truth. Arden begged me to stay, and I did, to be good, but it turns out she doesn't even need me anyway. Her power is the key, so she can find Mother on her own. I am so over trying to be good and feeling horrible about how little I measure up.

I'm not good. I'm not loveable. Not like Arden, who is more likely to be caught daydreaming with a book than starting an argument, who our family instantly falls in love with completely. I'm not the one whose power is going to save the world. I'm the bad twin—the one who talks too much, who never turns down, who's a liability when it counts. It's fine. It's time I got back to enjoying the best benefit of being bad: doing whatever I want to avoid feeling any hurt.

Tiffany walks toward us, her friend in tow, and immediately sizes me up. I don't know how, maybe she just senses through the queen bee cosmos that I'm down, but she asks, "You're cute, what's your name?"

Lilo, of course, butts in before I can even speak to Tiffany. "You don't talk to my cousin, Fanny. What you need to do is find another bus stop entirely and head there immediately with your tired ass."

"Leolidessa? Oh, here I was being polite and speaking to your guest. But I'm sorry, yes, let's pay attention to you! We all know how you might disappear otherwise." She winks at me, and I can't help but chuckle a little. Tiffany is my new favorite thing. "It looks like you're new in town?" she asks me, and I nod. She glances at me and Arden. "You two should come out raving with us tonight. I'm sure these sods haven't shown you anything fun."

For the first time since I stepped in London, I'm hearing someone talk my language. I take tiny side steps toward Tiffany.

"Fanny, my cousins aren't coming to your brother's trashy club, all right?" Lilo snarls. "Some people have respect for themselves, you see. Not that you know what that's like, but one day you might get there. Might I suggest a mountain rope?"

"Ooooh, nice one, Sis!" Liberty fist bumps Lilo. I inch even closer to Tiffany.

"Our bus is coming up right now anyway, so you don't need to spend any more energy being hostile or fabricating stories, all right?" The bus starts pulling up as Tiffany flips her hair and gives a final glance to me and Aurora. I see my chance.

"Do you think I could hang out with you guys for a while?" I ask Tiffany, my back to the cousins and Arden.

"Of course, I love showing new girls how we party. Let's go, cutie." She and her friend turn and start to board. I am right behind them.

"Rora! Don't go, please, we need to stay together!" Arden says, stepping up and grabbing my arm.

I shake her off. "Why?" I ask simply.

Tears form in her eyes. "What if something happens to you? I don't like this."

"You are free to continue in not liking this. But I am going. *Without you.*" I know she understands when the tears start falling down her cheeks.

I nod, acknowledging the intentional stab. There's this weird thing about making someone feel bad. It sometimes can make you feel better, bigger, more in control of your own stuff than they are. I board the bus, trying my hardest to feel all these things. I avoid looking out the window, focusing on the fun I'm about to have instead. I search through my book bag to upgrade my outfit, and I come upon Arden's passport, her smiling photo a stark contrast to the tear stained face I just left behind. When Tiffany passes her flask to me, I down the rest of it. It's time to numb away the pain I keep inflicting on everyone, including myself.

"Damn, my girl finished it. I guess you needed it, right?" Tiffany asks happily.

"Yes," I say gravely. "I needed it."

# 5

## *Arden*

## No Doubt

$\mathcal{I}$ have never doubted my mother's intense love for me, but I know that Aurora has, nearly every day of her life. We were six and on tour with Mom for *La Traviata*, in Italy, when Rora, wanting to wear a tutu, begged for us to be put in ballet class. We were only three weeks in when Mom didn't show up to collect us after our weekly class. Everyone cleared out of the studio, but Aurora and I waited with our instructor Mme. Cleary for nearly two hours. We called Mom millions of times to no avail, and Mme. was muttering to herself in Italian when Rora caught the words for "car accident." She started panicking, crying that Mom had died on the roads and now we didn't have anybody. We were orphans. Aurora raced out of the studio down the streets, still in her tutu, and I ran after her, also in mine.

I finally found her crying and sniffling against the wall of a gelato shop. "Aurora! Why are you crying? Why did you run away?"

"I just know Mom is dead and we're all alone!" she said, sobbing hard and gasping for air.

I sat next to her and held her tightly. "Mom is fine, she's just super late today, that's all! Maybe we should go back to the studio. Maybe she is there waiting for us right now, huh?"

Rora was still crying and hiccupping when we heard a voice behind us, "Are those my girls?!" We turned to find Mother coming out of the shop, dressed gorgeously in white, arm in arm with a handsome man. "I was just coming to get you two when I met Paulo here—why aren't you at the studio? What time is it?"

I embraced her, telling her I knew she was coming for us as always. I looked back, expecting to see Aurora's relief, but instead I saw heartbreak. Paulo offered her one of the ice cream cones in his hand, and in a quick fit, Rora grabbed both and smeared one on Paulo and the other all over Mom's white dress. She flung her tutu to the ground and took off running, back to the studio, straight into the bathroom, and slammed the door.

I followed, again. "Aurora, please come out."

"No!" she yelled through the door. "I hate her! She doesn't even care about us! She doesn't even miss us when we're not with her!"

"I . . . I don't know what to say, Aurora! I don't like when you're hurting, and I'm sorry. I wish today was different. I don't think she meant to forget us. I do think she loves us both. I really do!" I sat against the door and pressed my head towards the keyhole, hoping Aurora heard my sincerity. "But I'm here. I'm always here for you, and I love you so much. Will you come out, for me? Please?"

After a few minutes, my sister unlocked the door and

threw her arms around my shoulders, holding me tight. "Promise you'll always be there."

"I promise," I whispered.

Our tutu days were over, but Rora knew she could always count on me.

But ever since this morning, there's been a major shift between us. It's felt as though she's threatened by my passion for this quest and my connection with the cousins, like she doesn't believe I'm here for her at all anymore. I know my twin doesn't deal well with feeling overlooked. I know her fight-or-flight response is more akin to the scorched-earth theory. So honestly, given everything, Aurora's ghosting is no surprise. She's been hugely thrown by all this, so much more than me. To be honest, her reaction is at least a bit my fault, for not being a better sister. I've pushed her into this quest without ever really dealing with everything going on under the surface. She was trying to tell me how she felt this morning, and I just insisted we go to Gran.

I must have seemed dismissive of her and absorbed in the cousins and learning everything they could teach me. I've said a dozen times how much I love and need her for all this, but I knew my words just weren't sinking in. I sigh, thinking of the last thing Mom said, that Aurora and I must stay together. Well, now I feel like a failure as both a sister and daughter. How can I get my family back together now?

"Where are they going?" I ask, looking down the empty street. "We have to go get Rora back."

"Cousin, that's really in the opposite direction of Kiara's," Liberty says from behind me.

"Shit, Aurora!" I stomp my foot.

"I'd just like to take a moment to say, I called this," Lilo says casually.

I turn to give her an evil eye.

"Sorry, but I did! Your sis has been anti-everything since the moment you two landed. I know her type. I've met so many mean girls, I'm not surprised she ditched us for a shinier option. It's their M.O."

Liberty nods at Lilo's words but I can only hang my head in sadness. They don't know Rora. How can they judge her for reacting badly to the worst news of both of our lives?

"I know you want to go after her, but she so clearly doesn't want to be a part of this mission," Liberty says, squeezing my arm. "Maybe she'll come around eventually, but we really can't afford the time it would take to follow and beg her to join us right now. It'll take enough time for you to learn Kiara's power and locate your mom, and we're kinda on a time crunch . . ."

"Since our grandfather might kill Mom for fun any minute now? Yeah, I got the message clearly from Gran back there." I sigh again. "Okay, we'll go to Kiara's so I can locate Mom and make sure she's fine, but we need to get Aurora back. Can you try calling that Fanny chick?" I ask Lilo.

"I don't have that wench's number!"

I give her the evil eye again.

"But you know what, I'll reach out to my peeps and get it." Lilo starts texting as a bus rounds the corner toward us.

"Okay, Cuz. This is us," Liberty says, nodding toward the bus.

I step onto the bus and focus on mentally sending love and safety to both my sister and Mom, wherever they are.

"COME IN, FAMILY! Come into the warmth! Take off your shoes! Anyone for tea? I have those blueberry scones you love, Lilo. Come in, please." Kiara's voice is slightly more British than Jamaican, but a charming blend of both. When I take in her beauty, I have to remind myself to breathe. Her creamy light brown skin is perfection, glowing from within like a copper wire. Her face is a canvas for dramatic features: bright eyes framed by long lashes, high sculpted cheekbones, and a smile so wide and engagingly contagious, I feel my own lips rising in response. Kiara is wearing a simple tie-dyed tank dress with beaded fringe that swivels around her thighs as she walks barefoot around the loft.

I take off my shoes and jacket in the hallway, trying not to stare at this gorgeous woman. The place is hot like Gran Gran's house—the thermostat must be set to Tropical Island in both locations. The walls of the hallway are a robin's egg blue, scattered with colorful Caribbean art. The main room is huge and sectioned clearly, with a bed perched in a nook above the bathroom and the remaining space divided for an office, living room, kitchen, and a mini yoga studio by the window.

We gather in the light grey living room where Kiara brings us tea and scones on a tray, which Lilo grabs at immediately.

"I'm so glad to finally meet you, Kiara," I say wryly, lifting my hair off my neck and fanning myself for a bit of air.

"Thank you for having me. Your apartment is so pretty, and it's definitely warm in more ways than one."

"Oh, is it too hot? Let me turn on a fan!" Kiara switches the ceiling fan on and turns down the thermostat from the wall. "Goddesses are weakened by too much cold. I suppose though, I overdo it on the heat, but it makes me feel like I'm back at Gran Gran's, so . . . But please, let's sit and get comfortable!"

Kiara sits Indian style on a giant pillow across from us on the couch. She radiates confidence and positivity in a way that affects me profoundly. My anxiety and doubt are overcome by her calm presence. I can't explain why I suddenly feel better, until it clicks. This beautiful young woman is my cousin and *a powerful goddess*. Maybe it's the radiation the cousins mentioned, but the way her energy pulls me into her is like being enticed by a warm bath. I am in the presence of a goddess, and my whole essence wants to dip in.

*But you are a goddess, too, Arden.* I shake my head at the thought. I still need to prove myself and get my family back before I can fully believe that story.

"Kiara, we . . . *I* need your help to rescue my mom."

She smiles and nods. It's clear from her eyes that she knows already. Gran Gran must have told her why we were coming ages ago, like she did Lilo and Liberty.

But I still need to ask her officially now. "Please, could you teach me how to travel, to absorb some of your gift to find her?"

Kiara smiles and repositions herself. "I'm so glad that you are here, Cousin. My heart is open to your needs, and yes, I will do all I can to help you find your mother. Gran briefed me, and we have a plan. We can do this."

"Okay," I say, relieved.

Kiara smiles and nods. "Your mother's consciousness is imprinted within you. You're not able to reach her here and now, but if you focus and concentrate, and get emotionally closer to her, you could mentally zero in and transport to her to get the details on where she is held. Then we'll come back to our bodies here and rescue her as a group. Our grandfather won't let her go easily, so it's best we move in on him as one." She clicks her tongue and shakes her head in disgust. "This is a horrible thing that our grandfather has done. I have never met him, but I hear he is a terrible man . . . terrible."

"I know!" Lilo exclaims messily, a scone in her mouth. "All of this is scandalous! He put a hit out on his own grandson all those years ago, and then reappears now only to kidnap his daughter! Talk about being an anti-family man, man!"

"And Gran Gran is so wonderful, it's like, how did she ever get with someone who could end up becoming so evil like that?!" Liberty says, leaning in from the couch.

Our family skeletons are now laid out on Kiara's coffee table, and everyone but me is having fun picking at the bones.

"Guys?" I cough. "I hate to interrupt this, but my mother's kinda in danger this very moment, so . . ." I spin my index finger in the air, politely signaling for them to wrap up the chitchat.

Kiara catches me and chuckles. "She's cute," she says, to

Lilo and Lib like I'm not even in the room. "Is she always this cute?"

"Yeah, she's super cute, right? The other one's such a pain; you're lucky she's not here," Lilo supplies, shaking her head in disgust.

"That's my twin sister you're talking trash on!" I punch her in the arm.

"And? She's my cousin and a P-A-I-N. I stand by these words coming out of my mouth," Lilo says, taking a dramatic bow, flipping her purple braids in my face.

I roll my eyes at her and turn back to Kiara. I need to make her see how important this is to me. I hold her stare and push into her mind all of the worry and concern I have for both Mom and Rora. *Please help me help them. Tell me how to space travel*, I plead, and her eyes widen as she absorbs my mental signal of distress.

"Cousin, wow! Nice persuasive technique there! I feel what you feel for them." She shakes her head, "I love experiencing the incredible talent in our family! Okay, you win, topic shift to space travel for a newbie!" Kiara bounces on the pillow in excitement, then takes a long breath and looks at me all serious. "Warning label, I haven't mastered all facets of my power yet. I'm currently into some experimental stuff—teleportation and traveling on multiple frequencies to create multiple selves. It's what's causing the radioactive hiccups, but I promise we will not do anything too intense, just astral travel, not full on physical spacefaring, and definitely nothing on the exponential level."

I nod as if I know what she's talking about, even though I'm beyond lost.

"It gets easier and better with practice, but traveling to the astral plane is fully safe for your first time."

"Space travel virgin," Lilo whispers at me.

Kiara shoos Lilo away toward the kitchen and turns back to me. She gets up and sits on a yoga mat that was laid on the floor and indicates I should sit on her now available cushion. As I move to the seat, she starts explaining the process of transporting to the astral plane.

"It will take a lot of concentration and a buildup of potential energy to become an ethereal body, but it's not painful. It's more strenuous than anything, really. Once you separate your body and spirit from one another, you will appear as a phantom and can use your own powers to summon and follow your connection to your mom."

I'm trying my best to understand what I need to do, but her words fly past me and I'm lost as hell. My face must be as easy to read as ever because Kiara sighs.

"You didn't get that at all did you? Okay, I might not be explaining this well."

She looks up, trying to summon the answers from her mind, and I get an idea. "Just think it. Just think about it without trying to find the words," I tell her.

She looks skeptically at me, but Liberty nods from her place on the couch. "Trust her; she's got the weirding way," she tells Kiara, winking at me, and moving to join Lilo in the kitchen.

I look into Kiara's brown eyes and let myself melt into her thoughts. *Tell me about astral travel. How can I do it, too?* The room darkens around me and yet I am left with an image of Kiara sitting on her yoga mat with her eyes closed. In a moment I hear her voice ringing clearly in my head, though her lips never move.

*The difficulty of entering into any form of space travel comes from separating your mind from your body. The body does not easily release the mind, so you have to visualize pushing yourself mentally from inside out, forcing the disassociation, until you feel your body release your mind. Once that separation happens, you are in the astral plane; your body creates a hologram version of itself to move with your mind. No one will be able to see you; it's like becoming a ghost of yourself. But I'll be able to see you in the astral plane when I am there, also.*

I am still visualizing Kiara sitting calmly on the mat, but now I see a transparent spirit version of her slowly begin to escape, and then fly out of her body. *You essentially become a phantom in space*, she explains. *You can float and fly to wherever your mind focuses. We'll make sure your mind is focused on your mom throughout the whole process. The moment you are astral, we will travel to where your connection to her is pulling you. When you use your mindreading powers, we can get the info we need from her to rescue her. Then it's the reverse process to re-associate the mind back to your body.* The transparent Kiara smiles and bows slightly, then floats back into the sitting Kiara, the two becoming one.

"Ah, thank you, Kiara. That made a lot more sense," I say out loud.

She blinks at me in surprise. "So wait, you were just inside my head and got the information you needed?"

"Yes. You even did a demonstration for me," I smile at her.

"Wow, Cousin, I didn't feel anything! You can hack into brains and download information! Amazing mental powers."

She smiles at me in wonder, and I blush. "Okay then, are you ready to try space travel? It's the final frontier, baby." Kiara rubs her hands together like she's conjuring magic.

Learning is one thing, but doing? I'm immediately overwhelmed with doubt. I want to scream, "No!" What if something goes wrong? Should I really be testing a dangerous new power at this moment? *There's only now, Arden*, I think. *Your family needs you to be fearless.* I take a deep breath and smile at Kiara, pumping my shoulders up and down from my position on the floor cushion. "Let's do this," I say as confidently as I can.

She grins, pulling the cushion, along with me, closer to her yoga mat. "Okay, we'll sit and connect with our bodies and minds, then try to disconnect them. It will feel strange, but I'll be with you and talk you through it. And once you phantom, I'll be there. I can find you wherever you travel, so you won't be alone." Kiara smiles at me, and I forget why I was worried. *Everything is going to be fine,* she thinks into my mind, reaching out for my hands.

I close my eyes with her and concentrate on the feeling of my beating heart.

"Your mind and body are one. They are here and now," Kiara says aloud, her soothing voice coming softly but powerfully into my ears. "But the mind is elastic and can stretch beyond the body. Your mind is strong, Arden. Your mind is searching for your mother. Allow your mind to stretch, to reach toward her."

I feel a block and don't know how to remove it. If I am here and now, how can I get there, where Mom is being held?

"Breathe, Arden. Your body is the first barrier, but your mind can move past it. Find your mother, Arden."

I breathe in through my nose and out through my mouth, and I picture my mom, thinking immediately of her face, sad and worried as she held mine closely. The image was from the last moments we had together, and my heart sinks at the memory. But as I begin to picture her, I realize that woman is not who I need to find. Mom is more complex than Rora or I could ever have guessed. She had a family and a son and lost them tragically, but she chose to rebuild and become a mother again on her own terms. I think of her losing her voice for years, then finding the strength to sing powerfully again. Her resilience and courage inspire me. I love her. I miss her. I need her back. *Find your mother, Arden,* I hear inside my mind, the voice a mixture of my own and Kiara's.

I start to feel a tingling sensation spread through my body. It's like extremely aggressive tickling that makes me want to laugh and scream all at once, but instead I lean into the shocks, holding my breath and pushing my mind through and past my body, thinking of myself as the center of a banana, slipping slowly out of the peel. *Find your mother, Arden. Find her, find her, find her,* I tell myself. The tingle increases to a crescendo of constant shocks, and then I feel a final jolt, a punch that nearly knocks the wind out of me. I cry out as my mind stretches past my physical body.

Suddenly, I'm numb and cold all over with an overwhelming sense of lightness. I open my eyes and see that I am translucent, floating above the city with Kiara. *Hello, astral plane!* I think, both scared and proud that I am now an ethereal spirit. I look down at the lights and buildings along the River Thames. To our left is the London Eye. I think of how Rora would make a silly joke about Humpty Dumpty if we rode it together.

"Congrats, Cousin!" Kiara says. "I had no doubt you'd be able to become a phantom. Okay, stay focused on your mom. Think of her spirit—call out to it—until you can feel her mind pulsing back to you, when the mental connection opens up between you two and you can speak to her."

*Find your mother, Arden*, I think once again. I stretch my mind, concentrating on Mom, picturing her face, like a painting that shapeshifts in the light, smiling and mysterious and sad and joyful and secretive, all at once. Kiara and I hover over a row of buildings around the center of London, and I reach out, calling with all my heart, *Mom, can you hear me? Please?*

*"Arden? My love, how are you here like this? And why are you here? Are you okay?"* a weakened version of Mom's melodious voice echoes in my head.

*"Mom! I'm fine! I'm here to save you. We know you've been kidnapped. Tell me where you are!"* I push my mind into hers, following her voice in my head to get a vision from her mind. Slowly a picture forms: a wide, flat, white building. The sign on the glass siding reads "Museum of Cultural Art" with the address of the building. The image travels through the gallery, down a staircase hidden behind a wall, down a tunnel, and to a secret wing of the basement. I see blurs of men stationed here and there along the path till I see a locked room in the large kitchen where Mom is being held in a freezer.

*Oh no, they're draining Mom's powers!* I realize, taking in her spirit flickering with exhaustion.

*"I'm so sorry I left without telling you both the truth. Is Aurora okay, too?"* she asks, her words staccato from the cold.

*"Yeah, we're fine,"* I say, brushing past her actual question. *"Mom, you're literally tied up in a freezer! What have they done to you?"*

*"Oh, goons these days have no manners. They've drained my power and energy over the past few days, and I'm not sure how much longer I can hold on. But listen, you and your sister need to get away from here. These men are dangerous and they're trying to find you. I'm just bait here in the freezer—they want you to come for me. Please, save yourselves and go back home."*

*"You're not just bait, you're everything, and I'm not letting you go!"* I think fiercely. Doesn't she know it's her safety I'm afraid for, not my own? Her voice is so thin, as if she's barely holding consciousness. This terrifies me more than any threat from our grandfather's goons. All I can think is, *I need to get my mom out of there now.*

*"Arden, you and Aurora need to go back home,"* Mom says. *"I would give anything to see you again, but you need to get as far away as possible. You can't get in and out of this place without getting caught. They have me, but you can still be safe and live your lives."*

*"I am doing no such thing, Mom. I have come all this way to save you and that's what's happening."*

*"Arden, you really can't . . ."*

*"Mom, we both know you're too weak to fight me on this, so accept that you are getting rescued. Now sit tight while I scan your brain for more intel."*

*"I see I have no choice. Can I at least mention how much I love my talented and brilliant girls?"* Mom says, and I feel the pride in her thoughts. *"Whatever happens to me tonight, please remember that."*

*"Mom, we're going to rescue you. That's what's happening tonight."* I gently scan Mom's brain for images of her kidnappers, but I feel her jerk away as soon as I see a tall, handsome black man with a familiar smile.

*"Someone's coming, dear. I need to turn my energy to them, so they don't know we're in contact."*

*"Okay, Mom. We're coming for you soon. Stay strong."*

*"I love you, brave one. Please stay with your sister and be safe."*

Our connection fizzles. I look to Kiara, still floating beside me. "I found her! She's weakened, but she knows we're coming."

"Outstanding, Cousin! Now we need to reconnect these phantom selves with our bodies."

"Okay. How do we do that again?"

"Focus on the physical sensations back in the room," Kiara says, floating closer to me. "Connect your mind with what your body is experiencing there."

I close my eyes and begin to recall what my body felt before my mind escaped. The tingling starts, this time with more force than before. I remember the heat of the apartment, the rub of the corduroy pillow underneath my legs, and the rise and fall of my chest as I sit breathing. I squeeze my eyes tight against the pain as I feel the sting of my mind being pulled back into my body. I hear Liberty's voice saying, ". . . adult Girl Scout of Shame badges," and I feel the muscles of my face respond in a smile.

I open my eyes, and I am back in Kiara's loft, my head limp on my chest, sitting Indian style on Kiara's pillow. From the couch, Lilo and Lib look to me with concern.

"You okay, Cuz?" Liberty asks.

I smile to them and say, "It worked." I stretch my neck as I give Liberty the address of the building I saw, and she searches the route there on her phone. "Let's go save Mom," I say, trying to stand, but I fall back down, light-headed.

"Hold on there, tiger. It takes a lot of energy to do what you just did. You refuel, and let's plan this all out," Kiara says, rising gracefully to get some snacks from the kitchen.

"Mom is really weak," I tell Lilo and Lib, my heart racing at the thought of rescuing her. "I could hear and feel it. There's a bunch of guys protecting the place, including Grandfather. They've been keeping her in a deep freezer for days."

Kiara returns to the room with a Gatorade and a bowl of trail mix.

"Thanks," I say, twisting the cap off the bottle. I chug, then I continue. "First, we need to get Aurora. Her powers will definitely come in handy for disabling Grandfather at the art museum." I stuff a handful of trail mix in my mouth.

The cousins exchange a look of pain.

I swallow. "What?"

"We called around while you were out. Fanny is still at Monsoon but your sister . . . isn't there anymore."

"Okay, so where is Aurora?" I press, popping more trail mix in my mouth.

"We don't know," Liberty says, her eyes downcast. "No one seems to know where your sister is right now."

"What?" I ask, spitting out an almond.

"She, well, Fanny said on the phone, and I quote, 'Your cousin hooked up with some rando and left to get it on like a total slapper,'" Lilo says with a frown.

"End quote," Liberty supplies in a whisper.

"What?" I ask, a robot stuck on repeat.

"She and some random dude . . ."

"I know what you said, I just. . . are you serious?"

"Yeah, it's what Fanny said happened."

"No, I know you are serious. I just meant, like, I just can't believe this! This is crap!" I pick up a nearby pillow and slam it to the ground, angry beyond coherency about Aurora's newest move. It's poetic, really, how effortlessly she infuriates every inch of me. I *just* figured out where Mom is, so of course Aurora has to go completely off the map. Before I fully spiral into rage, my brain grasps at one hope. Reaching out toward Kiara, I ask, "Could I go back to the astral plane and try finding Aurora?"

She shakes her head sadly and crouches next to me on the floor. "I really wouldn't recommend you space travel again so soon, my love. The body suffers in releasing the mind, and we were out for a while. I would recommend your mind stay put in your body for the next twelve hours, no more astral plane for you tonight. And intake some more fuel, you definitely need it." She hands me an energy bar and pats my shoulder.

I growl as I chew, hating that she is right. Though my mind feels sharp, my body is still shaking. I drop my head into my lap, not wanting anyone to see the myriad of emotions overtaking me. My twin could not have picked a worse time to go off the rails. I am so mad at her, I could defend a thesis on all the reasons I want to execute her.

I mean, ugh! What am I supposed to do when my own flesh and blood insists on being so stubborn and selfish? How am I supposed to live with her being like this? "You can love her more than anyone," Leo once said. I laugh darkly now, wondering if his advice still stands. How do I love someone who ghosts when she's actually needed the most? Since our ballet days, I have always chased after her, calming whatever storm she's created. I close my eyes and breathe, trying to bring my heart rate down. I can't rescue or wait for her now. I have to do what needs to be done, for the both of us.

Emerging from my thoughts, I say, "Okay. We go and get Mom now. We're just going to have to leave Aurora. I don't . . . I can't . . . we have to proceed without her."

"It's the only choice right now," Liberty agrees. "We'll be fine doing this without her. Just before you came back to us, Lilo and I were talking about how the four of us will make an awesome tag team together." Liberty nods at her sister. "Listen, we'll make a big distraction by summoning all the animals we can to the area. Lilo and I will sneak in and unlock all the doors and turn off any cameras. Then you and Kiara can come in to help us take down any bad guys or booby traps set in place by Grandfather, by any means necessary. All goddess powers set to disarm, sedate, attack—whatever we need to do."

Kiara smiles, adding, "I'll travel from here and make multiples of me at the site. My black belt will serve us well when we're ready to knock them out."

I nod. "And I'm able to implant feelings and memories into a person, so I should be able to do the reverse to remove evil intentions. That should help us fix whatever's wrong with these guys that makes them follow our grandfather's plans."

"And what do we do when we run into Grandfather Ezekiel?" Lilo says, making fists with her hands.

"Leave him to me," I say. "It sounds like he's overdue for a hard wipe and reboot." Maybe it's the energy bars are kicking in, but I feel so buoyed up by my cousins' confidence and the astral travel success that I'm ready to take on Grandfather Ezekiel this very second. As soon as I get him to look at me, I'm going to erase every thought, every memory he ever had. It's the only way to guarantee he'll never harm anyone again.

Suddenly I get a vision of us executing our plan. I can see me busting into the museum with my posse, wiping Grandfather's evil mind, getting to Mom, and saving her from this mortal danger. "We're going to get Mom out of there," I say quietly. But just as the words come out of my mouth, I realize I don't completely believe them.

Because at the very last moment, anxiety and self-doubt rear their ugly heads inside me—confidence-shredding, toxic twins seizing my heart. *Aurora totally bailed on you . . . are you sure you can do this without her?* I look at my cousins and remind myself that they believe in me, that they have my back. *Yes, look how they are sacrificing so much for you, while also expecting so much from you, Arden. Are you sure you won't mess up and disappoint everyone?*

"Yes, we got this, loves! Can you feel the success just hovering in the air, waiting on us to seize it?" Kiara asks, throwing her arms wide and closing her eyes.

"I know! With Lilo and my army of fierce animals, the legion of kick-butt Kiaras, and Arden's mental sorcery work, we'll be unstoppable!" Liberty claps her hands, her eyes bright and hungry. "Think, in just a few hours, we'll have Grandfather knocked out cold and your mother back safely. Oh, this is going to be good." She flips her blue hair from side to side, "I love it."

"Yes, yes, yes! I'm so here for it!" Lilo shouts, rubbing her hand and shaking her shoulders gleefully. "'Goddess Force: Bad Guy Rehab. The Taking Grandfather Down Edition,'" she continues, throwing her voice like a film announcer.

Minutes later, Lilo, Lib, and I leave Kiara's warm apartment. As we start out in the chilly night, my heart thumps loudly. I pray for a share of the courage that my cousins have, to kill my lingering doubt.


THE NEW LONDON Museum is on a nearly two-block wide campus just south of the River Thames. It was previously known as the Mortimer Hospital, which was opened back in the early 1900s. Once renowned as London's pioneer institution for genetic research and testing, the enormous four-storied brick and marble teaching hospital closed in 2000 due to a scandal involving financial corruption by the board. Staff and services were transferred to newer hospitals, and the building, which includes secret tunnels to a soundproof underground wing, was auctioned off to a private real estate firm. The company renovated and rented it to a historical foundation, transforming the building into a museum showcasing antiques and history celebrating the multitude of cultures shaping London. The latest exhibit showcases antiques from Jamaica—because apparently the Fates love a good joke.

It's nearly two in the morning as we ride the bus to the heart of the city. We've got Kiara on one phone, and we're researching the art museum with another. Using blueprints we find online, we iron out our strategy for accessing the tunnels underneath the museum.

"I'm positive that Grandfather will have a whole bunch of armed mercenaries on his team, protecting him and whatever he's doing to your mom," Kiara says. "The aunts always said he traveled in a pack."

"Well, we'll be ready for them," Liberty says, her voice strong, determined. She zooms in on the map on her phone. "We'll break through the bottleneck here to get in to where he is hiding your mom."

For a moment, I'm left breathless. I met these people a handful of hours ago, and they're ready to walk into hell to rescue Mom with me. What did I do to deserve this generosity, this love? *It's what family does for family.* The thought comes to me as I watch Lilo giggle into the phone at something Kiara says. *They walk through whatever fire they need to for each other. Why can't Aurora feel it—that she's held by all this love, too?* My heart aches that she's not here, that she's just trying to avoid facing that we're goddesses, that she needs to put herself aside and be brave for Mom. Why can't she realize she's doing the exact same thing Mom did when she ran away so many years ago—tried to avoid the truth? It solved nothing then, and it helps nothing now.

"You got it, Cousin? Cousin!" Liberty bumps me back to reality.

"Sorry, what?"

"We'll use the birds to distract the guards and cut through them alongside the other animals we'll bring down there. You have to focus and get your mom out, no matter what. Find her and get out. And if you see Grandfather, don't even hesitate. Just melt his mind into mud."

"Here's our stop," Lilo says, clapping her hands like a kid who just arrived at the zoo.

"Kiara, we gotta go," Liberty says, ending the call.

We exit the bus and walk on the dark sidewalk down a street lined with quiet houses, toward the art museum. My heart is beating in my throat when we stop nearly a block away in a quiet, hidden corner between streetlights. Lilo texts Kiara that we are in place. Minutes later, four Kiaras surround us. They are dressed all in black, hair slicked back in a tight, low bun. Their suits nearly blend into the darkness. I poke the one closest to me and silently gasp when I realize she's all flesh and bones.

"You're amazing," I mouth to her, and she bows at me with a sly smile.

Lilo and Lib whip their index fingers in the air to signal that they have started summoning the animals. In seconds I hear the birds begin to gather in the street. I just barely see flaps of wings and bellies of white against the dark sky, but I feel the wind of hundreds of wings as they come to land in the grass, in the trees, and on the lampposts between us and the building.

"This is it, " I whisper to myself and the others. After a heavy look shared between the seven of us, we move in for a group hug, wrapping our arms around each other and mur-

muring at our shared bravery. When the Kiaras and I step back, Lilo and Lib transform into the two familiar black birds with neon feathers. They fly around our heads then take off toward the museum, where they will slip through an open air vent on the side of the wide building, headed down the path we traced on the blueprints, to the basement level and our grandfather's lair.

The Kiaras and I move to a small alley near the back entrance of the museum. There we squat behind a row of dumpsters to await the signal to move in on the building: a white bird singing "God Save the Queen." In this moment of stillness, I could drown in the waves of feelings crashing through me: panic, gratitude, power, doubt. It's taken so much to get here: the news that Mom is missing, the secret flight to London, discovery of our cousins and our powers, meeting Gran and Kiara—I have no idea how I'm still holding it all together, physically and emotionally. I breathe in through my nose and out through my mouth, ignoring the anxiety and rising nausea. Through the rush of emotions, I try to cling to a mantra, reminding myself that now is the time to be brave.

My ears strain to hear a bird's cry, but instead I catch echoes of a low and evil laugh coming from down the block. The rolling baritone stirs something inside me, and I shiver like an icicle has slid down my back. Mom would say, "Someone just walked on your grave," or in other words, someone wants you dead.

"Did you hear that?" I whisper to the Kiaras.

"No, nothing. Was it the signal?" one whispers back at me.

I rise and tiptoe forward. "No, it was definitely something else. A creepy laugh. I just have this feeling I should know that laugh." I'm now at the end of the alley looking out in the dark street. "I'll be quick, Kiara. I have to check this out."

"No, Arden, wait!" the Kiaras hiss. "It's time!"

Sure enough, the white bird appears above us, singing, leading us to the back entrance of the art museum. When I step into the street, a few yards away I see a hunched figure climbing into the backseat of a car. I waver for just a second—should I approach the car, or continue following the bird into the building? *Trust your feelings, Arden. Don't overthink it. You're a powerful goddess. Just be in the moment.*

"I'll be right back!" I yell to the Kiaras as I sprint down the street towards the car, my heart racing, charged by the sensation of knowing without knowing. *I'm right, I'm right,* I chant in my head as I push through the night air. I'm just inches away when the car's engine starts up, setting its lights aglow, as if it's coming alive. I slap the darkened windshield, "Grandfather Ezekiel," I shout. "You get out of this car right now!" The driver, a thin black man in dark glasses, ignores me, but the tinted back window opens several inches, and I hear the deep laugh emerge from inside.

"Ah, right on time. I knew you'd be arriving about now, Granddaughter. You'll forgive me if I don't face you," his voice sounds strong and amused, "but I know what you're capable of, and I do cherish my memories." The window slides up and car starts to pull away. I run alongside, slapping at the window.

"Stop!" I yell. But instead the car swerves at me, and I have to lunge behind a parked car to save myself. From the pavement, I hear a voice boom, "Goodbye, quiet storm!" as Grandfather's car drives away.

"Shit!" I yell, slapping the ground as I rise. I was just moments away from catching him; now who knows when we'll have such a chance again? "Shit!" I yell again, leaping up off the ground, running back towards the gallery. The Kiaras are already inside with Lilo and Liberty, and Grandfather knew we'd be coming all along.

"Stay far away from here, they want you, want your powers," Mom had said when I visited her. I know she wants to protect me, but as I run toward the fight, toward the danger, I finally feel free of any doubt that I am ready for whatever waits on the other side.

# 6

*Aurora*

## Don't Be Evil

*Two hours earlier*

*W*hen we were about eleven years old, while Mom featured in the Greek National Opera, we had a tutor named Doris. She was big on introducing us to fun games, including one called Oracle. Hidden within intricate folds of an origami structure were varying predictions of our future. Each turn revealed a potential storyline, and we let our imaginations run with it for days, the bright paper star thinning to pulp under our impatient hands.

Arden, with her enduring optimism, could find happiness in nearly any prediction. "My husband and I live in a shack with eight kids, and I'm a doctor? That's perfect, free health care!" or "I'm lost in the Bermuda Triangle with only a monkey and a Swiss army knife? Time to build a boat with Bobo!" she'd giggle.

Her eager glee was frustrating to me. I wanted only fortunes that promised me adventure and power. I hated the imagined burden of enduring a life with *any* children, much less eight of them. They'd require so much energy, attention, and care—even the thought of them felt stifling. Doris once caught me calculating results to land on "no children." She laughed while I grumbled, "If I didn't have kids running underneath me, I could be legendary."

"This will change when you're older, you'll see. You'll want to be a mama," she said, pinching my cheek.

But I knew myself then, and that truth has only heightened as I've grown. It's harsh, but true: I do not want to have children. Even further, I have never understood why people would want to have them.

Okay, of course I know biologically one thing leads to nine months and eighteen years of another, but really, why do people keep having kids? Don't they realize that children require constant sacrifice of your wants and needs for theirs? *My mother never got that memo, and apparently neither did Doris.* Despite the pounding music and pulsing lights, I'm lost in these thoughts as I stare with an open jaw at a super-duper pregnant chick getting it down on the dance floor. She's whipping her hair and shaking her hips, and I'm praying the baby won't make a grand entrance right here and now on the glittering floor. There are already too many birthday parties in progress as it is.

"Ugh, don't make me chunder, am I right? Does she, like, not know that we all can see her?" Tiffany says when she spies what's distracting me. "That's like the worst decision ever, showing up at a club pregnant—major cock up," she concludes, handing me another shot.

I take the drink, musing that getting pregnant in the first place was the truly bad decision, especially if you can't be bothered to slow down on partying. I bring my gaze to more appealing parts of the room. I am living inside a scene from a rap video right now, and I am absolutely loving every minute of it. We're at Monsoon, the club that Tiffany's brother owns, viewing the dance floor from the elevated VIP booth, flanked by a velvet couch and an unending supply of bottles of champagne, tequila, vodka, rum, and an array of chasers. The club is thick with bodies pulsing to the beat of the music.

"Come on, let's go dance!" Tiffany says, tugging my arm, pulling me down the short staircase. I join the girls in dancing and take in an amazing view of the city through the floor-to-ceiling windows across the dance floor—Buckingham Palace, the River Thames, and also the London Eye, the giant egg-pod Ferris wheel flanking the river. I feel a moment of weirdness at experiencing London without Mom and Arden. *Weirdness? Or shame, because you ditched them both even when they said they needed you?* a voice whispers through the haze of alcohol and dancing. I shake my head, determined not to spend any more brain power on Mother or Arden.

"Vincent!" Tiffany waves into the crowd. "He's my brother's friend. Hella reem, right?" she whispers directly into my ear to be heard over the music. I surmise that "reem" must means sexy, because that's the only word I can think of to describe the ridiculously handsome man joining us. He's GQ model material, and I'm drawn in from the moment he enters my vision. His skin is like smooth clay, his hair a buzz cut I know feels electrifying to the touch, his black button-down fitted enough to reveal an impressively built body. When I step closer, I am momentarily stunned by the subtle power of his cologne, a combination of cinnamon and overturned earth that makes my mouth water.

He embraces Tiffany, then pulls away and asks, "And who is this delicious carmellita?" His brow is raised in interest at me.

"Hey, I'm Aurora," I smile back at him with game-set-matched interest.

As I shake his hand, he holds and caresses my arm. He pulls me toward him and Tiffany melts away.

"Aurora?" he says, rolling my name around on his tongue. "Hmm . . ." He pulls on a strand of my curly hair and watches as it bounces back to life. I categorically hate when people touch my hair, *I am not your personal chia pet,* but in this moment, I find myself minding not one bit. He smiles. I smile. And everything feels good inside.

"You must know that the first Aurora was the goddess of the dawn?" He places his palm on my spine and suddenly we are pressed against each other and dancing intimately. "She commanded the sun to rise each morning," he whispers in my ear, his tongue just lightly grazing the lobe.

I shiver and try to steady my hazy brain. This dude is . . . so smooth, literally and figuratively. It's mesmerizing. His silk shirt feels amazing to touch, and my hand accidently finds a home in his soft buzz cut. He laughs, and I realize we are pawing each other to the music.

"I love the way you dance, Ma," he says seductively.

I feel wild, slightly out of my mind. "I'm sorry, I might have had a few drinks, and you're so . . . soft!" I catch myself in a giggle and hiccup. *Do I sound silly? Do I care? Should I? Where am I again?* My brain feels cloudier and foggier the longer Vincent and I dance. The song is changing when I realize he is holding up my entire weight and my shoes have slipped off my feet. *When did the room get so wobbly?* I wonder as I start to lose consciousness in Vincent's arms. The last thing I hear: Vincent's voice saying, "Good work, Fanny."

I open my eyes to darkness. I feel the heavy presence of others around me, their hot breath in the air, the shuffling of limbs, rustling of clothing.

"Who's there?" I cry into the room. I hear a snicker, a "shhh," and finally a voice whispers, "Turn on the light, Natalie, she's scared." A nightlight comes on, and after a moment, I can see around me. I'm in a room with a dozen rows of bunk beds, and staring at me from them are dozens of young girls.

Or at least they were once young girls. They look like people, but not normal ones and not in any condition you've ever heard about. Their faces are gaunt beyond measure; only their pale eyes and teeth are clearly visible. Their entire bodies are sunken in and nearly transparent. At first I think it must be a trick of the light, but then a girl turns to the side and I realize I am literally looking through her head. I suck in a jagged breath, and a ghostly girl to my right mimics the sound with a cruel laugh.

"Who are you?" I whisper.

Another snicker.

"We're imposters, posing as human beings," a voice from the back of the room answers me.

"What do you mean?" I ask, still huddled in the corner, too terrified to move.

"You'll find out soon enough. Vincent will come for you. They never let the fresh meat sit for too long."

My heartbeat pulses fast in my ears as I ask, "Who are they? Why are they keeping us here? What happened to you all?"

My voice breaks in fear, but the girls only respond with more snickering. A few shake their heads at me, sending waves of pity from their macabre forms.

"Look at her. She's so pretty. She won't be for long."

"What do they want?" I shout, but none of the girls answer me.

I start to get up from the floor when I hear a key unlock the door. The nightlight goes out in a breath as Vincent reaches into the room for me.

"No! What are they going to do to me?" I scream as he pulls me to out into the bright hallway.

A girl answers from the dark. "Take from you. And make you like us."

The door closes behind me. I'm shrieking and scratching at Vincent, but his iron hold is secure. "You creep, what did you do to me at the club? Let me go! I want to leave right now!" I scream at him. I channel the anger and adrenaline surging through my body and pull a florescent lamp down hard at Vincent's head.

He stumbles only slightly from the blow, but I pull out of his arms. I try to take off running when I feel Vincent embrace me again, his grip like a cobra, sucking the wind from my lungs. I'm struggling to move the next light with my mind when I feel a pinch in my arm; Vincent has injected me with a needle.

"Zion said you were a fighter," he says in my ear. "He's been waiting for your powers to craft his better world."

"How do you know that name?" I mumble, the hallway fading to black around me.

"He's our god," I hear just as I lose touch of everything.


THE FIRST THING I sense is the chill in the room. I'm sitting on a chair with my hands and feet bound tightly behind me. I open my eyes, but I can't see anything due to the darkness. I'm not with the ghost girls; I'm somewhere smaller and freezing: an ice box? *I'm really over this "funhouse of horrors" crap.* I try to channel my powers but feel nothing; the injection and cold are numbing my nerves. I shiver and hold back tears, sinking into a realization that I'm doomed. Whatever happened to the ghost girls is happening to me. My heart and energy level plummet. *I'm going to die here. I deserve this for being a horrible shit to my own sister and mother.*

I think about the mother I assumed was self-servingly choosing her career over us, then try to consider her with Gran Gran's insight—as a gifted goddess who loved, lost, and then rebuilt her entire life on her terms, a life filled with the determination to share the gift of her voice with as many as possible. Selene chose to be a mother again, even after losing her first child in a horribly tragic way. *Maybe she did the best she could for Arden and me,* I concede as scenes from the past flash through my mind. She could be distant and easily distracted by her fame, but I realize that deep down, our mother must have truly loved us fiercely to even have us after all she had already lived through.

One of the rare times Arden and I were sick as kids, Mother demanded a bed be brought to her dressing room so she could check in on us even briefly between scenes. At the time I thought she only wanted to heighten the drama of being a mother and star, but now I understand this was how she showed her love—by living her own life to the fullest and bringing us along, whether it be good, bad, or ugly. I've never given her credit for a thing, but I realize with stunned hindsight that she always tried to, and did, give us a wonderful life. The tears come heavily as I sit regretting every selfish move that led me to this chair, rope, and freezer prison. *I am a failure as a daughter and sister,* I realize starkly, replaying the events of the past few days. *Why do I see the worst in the people who love me the most?* My teeth chatter against my lips, and I whisper, "Cold, cold, cold," berating myself for a decade of foolish anger.

And then, I hear Mother's faint voice calling out, "Is that you, Rora?"

*Oh great, now I'm hallucinating!* I gasp and cry harder, barely able to breathe.

"Don't cry, my darling. I'm sorry. I'm all tied up over here and can't move. Is Arden here too?" Mother says.

My heart leaps. *She's here! Not just a disembodied voice, but actually here in the freezer with me!* "Mommy? Is it you? You shouldn't be here!" I cry out, turning in the direction of her voice at the opposite end of the room.

"No, *you* shouldn't be here," she sighs sadly. "I should have warned you. I played the fool to think I could keep you and Arden from this forever. Where is she? Is she safe? She contacted me earlier; I thought you were together somewhere safe. What are you doing here?"

I think of my trusting, loving twin, and start crying even harder. "I . . . I don't know. I left her. I'm sorry, I'm so selfish and horrid and now I'm here and I can't help you or her and something really bad is going to happen and everything, everything is my fault." I'm sobbing, the cold air blasting into my lungs.

Mother shushes me from across the room, "No, shhh, baby, nothing is your fault. This tsunami of a mess started from the winds stirred centuries ago." She sighs jaggedly. "These men are evil with dark intentions. I don't even know where to begin to explain."

"Our grandfather," I whisper, barely able to calm myself. "He and some guy named Vincent kidnapped a bunch of girls. They've done something really terrible to them."

"Yes, your grandfather's a part of it. I wish it were only him we needed to defeat. He lured me from home, under threat of harming you two, and I thought I could handle him. I had no idea about the Brotherhood."

"Wait, the Brotherhood?" I ask, straining my body in the direction of her voice. "What do you mean?"

"Yes, that's what they call themselves. There's at least a dozen of them, followers your grandfather has assembled. Their leader has the terrifying ability to feed off of women, absorbing their life power and abilities, and then sharing that power with his followers."

"What? Feeding?" I say, startled. "Wait, they're eating the girls alive?"

"Essentially, yes. Draining their souls and bodies dry, over and over. They have three dorm rooms back there filled with women they've kidnapped and abused. The Brotherhood are preparing for something big, and they've been talking about you and your sister obsessively." She pauses and her next sentence comes out in a whisper that I strain to hear. "I'm very scared for you, Aurora. I really wish you weren't here, baby."

In her shaking voice I hear the truth: She would give anything to take me away from here right now. I close my eyes and release the sins I've been carrying against her. "Mom," I say, "I have been an evil demon child. I was so mad at you for leaving us. I was furious that you lied about our whole lives, your whole life, everything. I just snapped. I didn't want to find you, even when it was clear you needed help. I am so very horrible. I left Arden, I got drugged and kidnapped. I don't even know what else to say. I'm selfish and useless and sorry, so sorry. I'm so sorry." My lungs heave, burning as the freezing air pumps in and out of my chest. I think of Arden's face as the bus drove off, and I cry harder.

"Oh Aurora," Mom says. I can hear her crying from the other side of the freezer. "I know it's not easy being my daughter, being your special self, with or without powers. But listen and know that I've loved you and wanted everything good for you since the moment I found out I was pregnant with you two. I wanted a life of freedom for you and Arden—for you to see the world, to be independent and spirited women, to learn to love life fearlessly. I thought if we kept moving, I could keep you safe. I made a binding spell on your powers to protect you. I tried frantically to keep the lid on the cage, but trouble found us anyway. I'm sorry I've told you so many lies, Aurora. What good is a goddess if she can't seem to do right by her own children?" Mom takes a jagged breath, "I had a son many years ago . . ."

"Zion? Yeah, Gran Gran told us he was murdered," I whisper.

"No." She breathes deeply. "I thought he died. I was wrong."

Suddenly, the freezer door opens, startling us both. Light spills past an impressively built man blocking the doorway. "Don't beat yourself up too hard there, Mother," he says smugly. "It's not the first or last thing you'll get wrong in this lifetime."

He turns to smiles contemptuously in my direction, and my jaw drops. We share the same light brown eyes and dimples. I recognize that crooked grin from the baby photo hanging at Gran Gran's. "Zion?" I whisper.

He nods, smirking at me. My brother, who was murdered nearly a century ago, is very much alive.

"And hello, baby sister Aurora. I believe one of these is yours, but I assure you, you have no need of it anymore." He throws Arden's and my passports at my feet.

I say nothing.

"Why are you so quiet? Shocked I know which twin is in front of me? I heard you were pretty wild at the club, right? So easily enticed away from the cosmic protection of your guards by a little night out in London. Only the wild twin, Aurora, would leave in such a selfish display. But, like mother like daughter, eh?"

I ignore Zion's taunts but wonder what he meant by cosmic protection. My mind blanks till I remember during our goddess cram session, the cousins mentioned we needed to stay together for safety. That they were our protectors. They were showing off their quartz necklaces at the time, and I thought they were just being dramatic, but were we literally under their protection? And I walked away. Into this. Wow, I suck so much I should get a medal.

"You know, I'm really annoyed that I'm not seeing double of you right now," Zion says, sucking his teeth. "Aurora, you don't know much about me or grandfather, but let me tell you one thing. We really hate any single bit of incompetency when it comes to executing a plan."

"What plan?" I ask softly. "Why are you doing this?" I look to Mother and see that she has passed out. "Just let us go," I plead. Like Arden, the smart one, would.

"See, I can't let you go. I've waited too long as it is, baby sister. It's finally time."

"Time for what? I don't understand any of this."

"Of course you don't. Grandfather prepared me for the lack of understanding, as well as the disappointment I would have to navigate. Like, when you say, 'I need to consume a girl and her doppelgänger at exactly midnight,' and your trusted followers say there will be no problem, but then they just deliver the shitty clone one, what are you to do other than kill them?" He shrugs. "The rest of the Brotherhood understand better now, that there is no room for failure, not tonight. I've got most of them on watch for your sister. Any moment they'll have her. I guarantee she'll be here very soon."

"You leave her alone!" I growl and fight against my ropes, but Zion's smile only grows wider. "What are you on?" I yell at him. "Let me and Mom out of here! You're my brother. What the hell are you doing? What is wrong with you?"

"Nothing is wrong with me. You don't understand. I'm a god, you see. I'm perfect . . ."

"Wrong!" I yell out.

"I'm what the Fates should have sent to tame the earth, all those years ago," Zion continues, squinting his eyes at me. "Powerful women are a mistake, and goddesses are an abomination. All you can do is make a mess. Didn't Mother just admit to that exact thing? She's pathetic. Look at all the trauma and war and turmoil in our world, and where can she be found? Singing at the opera house! I'm here to save the world that has been destroyed while the so-called goddesses have done nothing. It's okay, baby sister. I will fix everything, with your sacrifice. And I want you to know it's not personal. It's necessary. After tonight, after I drain the power from you, your sister, and our mother, there will be nothing that can stop me in remaking the world as it should be."

I'm itching to kick his face in or use my powers to hurl this chair at him, but all I can manage is spitting a wad that hits his shoulder. He laughs and takes off his jacket, throwing it at me. I shrug it off my face angrily.

"Ghani saw you clearly, and Grandfather and I did our homework. Arden's the lover; you, Aurora, you're the fighter. Not that it'll save you tonight, fire starter."

"How would you know about Gran Gran's visions?"

"That fool Ghani? Grandfather . . . he should be here any moment. He knew from the moment she became a goddess that nothing would be right in the world. He has worked, waited, and planned for a way that the balance could be restored. Tonight all of his efforts will pay off.

"I don't even know if you can appreciate the genius of our grandfather. He came to this place many years ago when it was still a research hospital. He worked with the genetic scientists, secretly experimenting with Ghani's blood, eventually creating a serum that granted him access to listen in on her meetings with the Fates. When he found out that Selene was pregnant with twins, a boy and girl, he began feeding her a concoction that made me stronger until my sister was absorbed into my body."

"Oh my god, no," I gasp, straining against my bonds. I've heard about fetal resorption, a natural biological maneuver that happens during some twin pregnancies. I'd even taunted Arden about it once, telling her, "I should have absorbed you while I had the chance." But this was induced. This was murder. Grandfather turned to science to craft a grandchild into a weapon for his own revenge against the Fates.

"Through Grandfather's intervention of my birth, I became a conduit, able to absorb power from women. We've waited for your powers to ripen, and tonight, you and your sister will surrender them to me."

"So it's our grandfather who feeds you all this chauvinistic horseshit? That you deserve complete power?" I scream, remembering that Grandfather Ezekiel was a part of a group who wanted to subjugate women's power centuries ago—that he was willing to kill his own daughters for even a hope of grand control. "You are both sociopaths! We're supposed to be family!"

Zion laughs darkly and begins pacing in front of the door. The freezer switches from darkness to light each time he walks in front of the single light on in the kitchen. "You're just a young girl," he says, his voice low. "You haven't seen, don't know half of what I know about how the world really works—its constant corruption and suppression of the strength and potential of the black man. You have no idea how it was for me growing up back then—the racism, the hatred I constantly felt. And then once my powers took hold, how I could feel the way white men wished for my death, threatened by nothing more than my mere presence. And it's so much worse everywhere else! God, we can't even begin to talk about all that's happening in America! But I will fix all of it and put the black man back in his seat of power. In just a few minutes, you'll die, but I'll absorb your full powers and put them to good use, forever. You know, you should actually thank me for making your abomination of a life worth something."

I feel myself inflamed, thinking of the ghost girls, their transparent skin and sad, hollow eyes. They are all suffering because my brother and grandfather share some fermented misogynistic delusion of grandeur?

"It wasn't evolution," I say. "It was evil science, drugging and murder. You need to be put down, Zion. You're nothing but a disgusting thief, robbing what belongs to those weaker than yourself. How can you even look in the mirror?" I once thought I was evil and was scared to look myself. But now, and here, in the face of the most horrifying actions of another, I realize I am definitely closer to good than I ever gave myself credit for being.

Zion folds his hands across his chest. "You would do well to show some respect to me while you are still alive."

"You're not a god; you're not even a man. A true man supports all women and protects his mother and sisters, even if they have strength that rivals his. Because in the end he is never looking to fight against them but *with* them. I'm sorry if our mother disappointed you, but you've become a pathetic excuse for a man. How can you believe that this horrible plan is the path to a better world? I will not let you kill me today or any day. And I'll make you pay for what you've done to those girls and Mother."

In that moment, I feel it, the fire moving through my body that means my powers have activated. My mojo is back. I use my powers to snap out of my bonds. With my mind, I slam Zion backwards against the freezer door. His body hits it with such force it breaks off its hinges, and Zion winds up stunned on the floor in the dimly lit kitchen.

"Mother!" I yell, tearing her bonds off and throwing her arms around me. We limp out of the freezer, me supporting her barely conscious body, and I realize Zion is no longer on the floor. I can't see him anywhere. Mother and I move along a long, stainless steel counter, then duck when we hear a scream echo in the distance. Someone fires a gun twice. Then we hear more shouting and slamming, and then a lion's roar and a bear's growl. The cacophony continues. I wonder what the hell is going on, but just as we approach the open kitchen door, Zion appears in front of us.

"Leaving me for a second time, Mother? For shame, for shame," he sneers and reaches toward us to grab Mom's throat.

I send him flying back against the wall, but he rebounds quickly, pulling a painting off the wall and throwing it toward us. I stop the painting in midair and send it boomeranging back at Zion. He dodges it with superhuman speed. In a blink he is gone from sight.

"Are you okay, Mom?" I ask.

She murmurs weakly as I hitch her weight under my arm and steer us to the hallway, but Zion appears again in front of us.

"Where do you think you're going, baby sis? It will be midnight and your last birthday very soon. And . . ." He smiles in a devilish way. "I'm excited to announce our final dinner guest has arrived. She's here, finally. I know how you teens love to be fashionably late."

"Arden!" My heart jumps. It must be her and the cousins making all that noise in the hallway. *Arden, please be safe.* I think, sending out my love to her. *I'm so sorry about everything. You were right, Mom needed us, and I should have gotten my shit together from the jump. I should have been fighting with you, not against you.* I hated on her for being so steadfast and good, but I am so damn proud of her for following through, despite all the odds. She fought so hard to find Mom. I didn't want to see it before, but all along she's been fighting hard to love me, like a true sister would. I only pray she won't get hurt trying to rescue me and Mom. *Please be safe, Arden.*

*"Aurora! I hear you!"* Arden's voice comes in through my

head, and only Zion's menacing gaze keeps me from shouting with joy at the sound.

*Arden! It's working, your voice is in my head, your telepathy works on me!*

"I'm coming!" Arden says.

*You need to leave, Arden. It's our brother. He's alive, he's evil, and he wants to consume our powers at midnight. I'll explain more later, but I need you to do something now. There's three rooms full of girls who have been kidnapped and abused, just down the left hallway. You need to get them out of here. Don't worry about Mom and me; I'll hold Zion off, but those girls need rescuing now.*

"Okay, stay strong sis. I'll free the girls, but I am coming for you and Mom next."

*I'm sorry I've been such garbage to you. And everyone.*

"Hold your apology for when I save you, loser," Arden responds, and I can't help but smile at how much I love her.

"Is there something amusing about your impending death, sister?" Zion asks me.

"Riddle me this, Zion. If you are our grandfather's truest disciple and most steadfast believer in the cause and blah blah whatever, where is he at now? Huh? How come he isn't here at your side, watching your triumphant rise to power?" I taunt him, shrugging my shoulders.

Mom, finally fully awake, and picks up the conversation. "Yeah, I haven't seen him much since the first day I got here, Zion. You'd think he would be here right now, by your side, if it is really what he wants," she says.

"Of course, this is what he wants!" Zion snarls. "I have done everything he has ever wanted, every step of the way. I have become exactly who he wants me to be. I know he'll be here any moment now. Tonight is following his plan precisely."

"Are you sure about that?" Mom asks. "From where I'm standing, it looks like he couldn't be bothered with what happens next."

"Yeah, from what I hear," I add, "he's not that into loyalty. Maybe he realized you're a sorry excuse for a leader and dipped out before you became a total embarrassment."

Zion strides forward and slaps me hard across my cheek, slamming me down to the floor in the process. He picks Mom up by the throat, and my own ears are buzzing as I struggle to stay conscious.

"Your time has long passed, Mother. It's time I put away childish things, and that includes any concern for you."

I flinch as Zion strangles Mom, but then see Lilo behind Zion, morphing from a black bear back to a human. I have never been as happy to see her as I am the moment she body-slams my brother. Surprised, he lets go of Mom and turns to the now tiny goddess behind him.

"So, you came back from the dead just to kill your family, Cuz?" Lilo shakes her head at Zion. "That's like, super morbid, you know."

I grab Mom away from the fray and pull her into the kitchen as Lilo laughs.

"Who are you?" he yells, punching the air as Lilo gracefully dodges him. "I want you dead!"

"There no reasoning with a dick, am I right?" she says, throwing her knee into Zion's groin with the force of a truck. He groans and doubles over, falling to the floor with an unconscious thud.

"All right Lilo!" I cheer, and the three of us quickly set to tying Zion's limbs together with the rope I pulled off Mom. We prop his body against the kitchen wall.

"Mackenzie is going to be so mad she missed out on all this fun. We've got twelve guys knocked out and tied up in a room. Arden just led out a bunch of girls from some rooms out back. We are killing this rescue mission!" Lilo says, dancing on tip toe around Zion's slumped frame.

"I'm just glad she's safe," Mom sighs.

I'm nodding in relief when suddenly Zion's watch beeps loudly. With a start he comes to, wrangling me to the floor. Mom and Lilo scream and grab at him, helpless against his snake hold on me.

"Happy birthday, sister," he says, squeezing my head between his hands.

I feel a wave of nausea rush through me as Zion inhales, sucking the power from my body. Mom's and Lilo's screams are mute to my ears, as they try to pull his arms and drag me away. After a second, I feel waves of weakness throughout my body. I look into Zion's eyes, and I see the fire and life that I once saw in my own.

"Let go of my sister!" a voice pierces my foggy grasp on consciousness. *Arden!*

Zion turns to her, losing his grip on me. *Maybe, just maybe I'm not evil, but she's definitely the good twin. Definitely.*

As he lets go of my skull, I fall to the floor limply, gasping for breath. And then I see Arden. She's standing in the doorway, glowing, much bigger than herself. Her whole being rings with strength as she glares into Zion's eyes and walks toward him. She could probably melt his brain, but I know she won't kill him. She's going to use her powers to make Zion good again. *Because Arden uses herself to make the world a better place.* Just before I pass out cold, it clicks: *And that's why people have children.*

# 7

## *Arden*

## HAPPILY EVER AFTER

The phrase "happily ever after" has always felt like a cop out of gigantic proportions to me. The dragon has been slayed and the princess rescued from the tower, but does that guarantee peace? Even when the dust has settled, can we rely on things to be okay from here on out?

Against my closed eyelids, I see a small boy being awakened from bed, made to recite from a handwritten book. His face is slapped by an older man, Grandfather Ezekiel, any time he begins to fall back to sleep. I see the boy being whipped by his grandfather, biting his tongue so he won't make a sound. The boy writes a letter to his mother, but he's caught by the grandfather, forced to drop the paper in a fire. The boy grows cold to his mother, aunts, and grandmother as the intimidation and abuse continue for years behind closed doors. *I'm sorry, Zion.* I push deeper and see that the hurt, confused young boy is still alive, layered behind a trumped-up, sadistic alpha male persona built by our grandfather.

"What are you doing to me?" Zion cries, his body writhing in pain against the floor. "Stop!" he yells, but I place my hands over his forehead and chin, steadying his head and smoothing his brow with my thumb.

"Yeah, this won't be fun. I'm wiping your brain, brother. Since your childhood you have been a host to horribly malicious thoughts planted by our grandfather. He's made you into an evil man, but his hold over you ends now."

I close my eyes to Zion's screams and focus on the humanity of the little boy inside him. *I see you, Zion. I'm going to help you through this.* I push through Zion's mind, fighting through layers of consciousness, powerfully binding most of his memories, and grinding my teeth so as not to cry out from the intensity of emotions. Underneath the hate, woven in with blinding anger and cutting insecurity are fierce pain, cold neglect, and heavy confusion. *Come out! You deserve to live and love,* I say to Zion's true soul.

*"But I don't like being alone!"* he cries in fear. *"I belong with Grandfather. I have to do what he wants, be what he wants, or I'll be alone."*

I shake my head. *You belong with the people who love you and want nothing but to show you that.* I unlock Zion's childhood love for Mom and Gran Gran and shine it like a beacon through the fear and doubt inside his mind. I see the little Zion growing stronger and bigger, the darkness that was suffocating him falling away. Soon the flesh and blood Zion is breathing calmly.

"I think it's okay now," I say, rising from the floor, my head slowly clearing to the world around me. I exhale slowly, trying to release the negativity that transferred to me from Zion.

"Arden!" Mom yells from behind me.

I help Aurora onto her feet. Mom wraps her arms around the two of us.

*"Arden, you saved us,"* Aurora thinks.

I cradle her cheek, thumbing away a cold tear. My other arm squeezes Mom close, and I inhale her deeply, the scent of Chanel and strawberries flooding me. I am awash with calm. My heart is home.

"Whoa, you have some of Mackenzie's happy float going on!" Lilo says, and I realize the three of us are levitating off of the floor. *I didn't know we could even do that.* We laugh happily, slowly untangling ourselves and landing back on the ground.

Just then Liberty runs through the door with one of Kiara's doubles. "Yes, you guys look well chuffed! Hi, Auntie! I'm Liberty, and this is Kiara, kind of. I'm happy to announce that all the naughty boys have been put to bed!"

"Yeah," Kiara smiles. "Arden erased all their memories and we locked them up in a bedroom to sleep it off. Without their daily supply from Zion, they'll soon lose their super strength and speed."

"Get over here everyone! I can't believe how wonderful you young goddesses are!" Mom says tearfully, reaching out for us. "Thank you, thank you for everything."

"What about Grandfather?" Aurora asks from inside our giggling group hug.

"He got away," I say, grunting at the memory. "Just before we broke in here, I saw him take off with some man."

"My older brother, Teresh," Mom sighs. "I heard them talking. He was in on this terrible scheme, too. They're cowards. Teresh wouldn't even face me. He and father probably ran off to wait for the fighting to end and Zion to appear victorious."

I'm about to ask where she thinks they could be, but Aurora interrupts.

"And what happened with the girls they were abusing?" Aurora asks, looking to me.

"Oh, we got all three rooms of girls released," Kiara responds. "They helped us fight off the steroid dudes, but then scattered throughout the hallways."

"They wouldn't follow us in here. Said they prefer to stay in the dark," Liberty shakes her head sadly. "They're in really bad shape, Aunty. And still they fought with us, bravely. But now they need our help."

My heart drops.

Mom nods her head, "We need to get them out into the moon, by the water," she says, her gaze focused on the door. "You leave it to me."

Mom walks out the kitchen door toward the hallway and begins to sing, her voice growing strong and dynamic. Lilo transforms herself into a horse, and we roll Zion's frame across her back, following Mom as she weaves throughout the compound. Drawn by Mom's song, slowly the ghost girls gather, and together we parade outside, under the full moon. The girls remain transfixed as the hauntingly beautiful aria leads them toward the river with a song about healing, sisterhood, moonlight, and change.

Once we reach the bank, Mom guides the ghost girls into the water up to their shoulders. The rest of us remain on the grass, watching a wave move through the river, surrounding the girls. The wave bubbles and splashes, and in a moment, the girls are surrounded by a crowd of strikingly beautiful mermaids. Slowly they emerge from the water, and Aurora grabs my hand as we both look on in amazement. The mermaids' hair is tangled with seaweed and shells in every texture imaginable, their skin a family of colors from blue, green, to purple. The curves of their bodies glow iridescently in the moonlight. They begin singing along with Mom, circling the girls serenely. The notes of the aria crescendo, and the water bubbles into a rainbow of colors. The ghost girls begin to shake violently and fall one by one, splashing and convulsing into the water.

Aurora gasps and lunges forward to help, but I hold her back.

"No. This is good. The water, song, and moonlight— they are creating a tonic. They're bringing the girls back to life." I smile, hugging my twin.

Sure enough, moments later, the girls start to emerge, walking up the river bank. They are full bodied, beautiful, and healthy, their skin and eyes glowing with life. *Like they deserve to be.* My eyes tear involuntarily as I watch the girls embrace each other.

I look at Zion's limp body and wonder what ending he deserves? What does he need? After a century of the manipulation and bad deeds, all I know is our brother needs a lot of help.

We watch the mermaids slip gracefully away in waves. As Mom walks towards us, I embrace her. "Mom, you're amazing," I whisper in her ear. She shakes her head, but I persist. "Look, we just watched you summon mermaids and heal the sick. You can't play the fool with us anymore, okay?"

She smiles and kisses the top of my head then reaches her arm out to pull Aurora into the embrace. "The mermaids and I bonded many years ago. My best friends growing up were mermaids. I knew I could count on them to help heal these girls tonight."

*Goddess daughters of the moon and sea*, Gran said. Mom squeezes me, and I have a flashback to a mermaid saving Aurora from drowning when we were kids.

Kiara approaches us and bows to Mom. "That was such a spiritual experience. I am blessed to be a witness to your healing, Yemanja." She turns to Aurora and me, "I am so glad I was here for that, but I need to get back and re-form. I love you all—let's catch up soon, okay?" She blows a kiss, then in a blink, Kiara is gone.

"Where did she go?" Aurora gasps, and I smile knowingly.

"Back home to her actual body. She space traveled and created multiple selves here to help us fight," Liberty replies.

Aurora scoffs, "What? Is that even possible?" She shakes her head. "You know what? I don't care. Everyone deserves a round of applause for however you made this rescue happen. Now I'd like to know how we're going to get dozens of girls and an unconscious man on a horse out of this place quietly."

"Does one of you have a cellphone?" Mom asks. Liberty hands hers over. Mom punches a long series of numbers, then asks, "Leo? Yes, I'm fine, I have the girls. You need to come here. London. Our son is alive."

Arden and I gape at each other.

*Leo is Zion's father!?* I think to Aurora.

*"I should change my name to Blindsided, because I did not*

*see that coming,"* she responds. We listen as Mom gives Leo our location and tells him to send a private bus.

"I love you, too," she says, hanging up the phone and turning to us. "Leo is sending a bus. Arden can clean the girls' minds and we'll drop them off at a police station, then head to Gran's. I haven't seen my mother for years . . ." she muses distractedly, patting her hair.

"Mom, wait, Leo—our godfather Leo—is Zion's father?!" I ask, my voice rising. Mom starts up the hill towards the street and calls the girls to follow her.

"Oh, that. Well, yes, Leo is the best man I've ever known, and he was my first great love. His family of minor deities always quarreled with Father, and we lost touch after Zion died—well, after we thought he died. But when I had you two, he came back into my life as my oldest and dearest friend." She frowns at my involuntary bounce of joy. "We're not in love anymore, Arden, do you hear? But honestly? Okay, we love each other. I've always loved him, of course. When my sister Annikay was pregnant with Lilo, she was looking for a name that summoned strength, wisdom, and a great capacity for love. I was the one who suggested the name 'Leolidessa.' But we're just friends," Mom says.

As I bounce up the hill beside Mom, Aurora catches up to me and whispers in my ear, "Wow. Situation update, Leo is the love of Mom's life and a minor diety!"

"Wait," I grab Mom's wrist, "is he our real father?"

"No, please Arden," she swats me away, playfully. "I would have told you that."

"Oh, yeah, you have such a great track record of honesty, Selene, or is Yemanja your name today?" Aurora teases and Mom blushes.

"Okay, point taken. But no, Leo is not your father. He is Zion's father and your godfather only."

"But is our father really some married director of the symphony who wants nothing to do with us? Or is there some deity-laced mystery there, too?" Aurora presses.

Mom holds her temple as we near the street. "Aurora, let's talk about this later, please. The bus will be here any moment now."

"It's a yes or no question, I don't understand—" A low honk echoes from around the building.

"The bus is here!" Liberty yells, skipping as she leads the girls and Lilo and Zion up the road.

"So, there is something I've been meaning to tell you. Happy birthday, girls," Mom says, wrapping us tightly in her arms. "I love you two beyond measure."

"Aww, yeah!" Aurora squeezes my shoulder, a wide smile spreading across her face. "We made it to eighteen! And we're all together! Happy birthday, Sissy!"

"Happy birthday, Twinsie," I say, and we giggle and rest our foreheads together for a moment. *After everything, I have my mother and sister back!*

"Eighteen years. How could it be so long ago, when it feels like only today I welcomed you to the world?" Mom sniffs.

"What made you change your mind after Zion? Made you decide to have Arden and me and be a mother again?" Aurora asks, biting her lip as if she regrets the words the minute they leave her mouth. We both stare at Mom.

"Because," she says, brushing away tears. "I knew you would make the world and living in it that much brighter. After a while on my own, I realized my life wasn't complete without being a mother. And when I got pregnant with twin girls, I knew this would be the best part of my life, forever."

"I love you Mom. I don't say that enough," Aurora says, her eyes welling with tears. "I'm sorry that I'm so much to deal with sometimes. I don't mean to be. I just . . . I'm going to try to be better. And I'm sorry I forced us to live in Ohio, it's probably how Grandad was able to track us down, right? And it's not how you want to live. We can go wherever. As long as we're together, that's all I really need."

I stare at Aurora. She's different now. Her heart is cracked open and love and compassion are spilling out. And it's gorgeous.

Mom holds Aurora's face in one hand and pulls me close with the other. "I love you two more than anything. I'm so proud that you had the confidence to take on this impossible quest and rescue me. You inspire me." She sniffs and the tears fall in earnest. "From now on, honesty, always, and the best of me. From goddess to goddess."

"Aww, Mommy," I say, and my heart melts at the sincerity in her voice. Like pieces of a human puzzle, we fit our limbs together, promising to be our best for each other and ourselves. *Has my heart ever felt this full?* In this moment, with Mother, daughter, and daughter in a trinity of bliss, I do indeed believe in happy endings.

.ڡلوڡ.

I WAKE WITH a jolt the moment our bus pulls up to the curb in front of Gran Gran's house. I take a deep breath to clear my fogged mind, recalling all that has transpired. The girls were bussed to a police station, their memories of trauma and recovery wiped, eager to reunite with their families. Zion awoke, revealing his true self, a quiet but lighthearted person. We helped him understand what had happened, and he accepted that his memory loss, while permanent, was for the greater good. Now I look out the window and see Leo racing out Gran's front door. I blink—*Could this be a dream?* But it's truly him, here in London. He's near frantic as he bounds up the bus steps, scanning the rows of seats. The moment his eyes land on Zion, he falls apart, sobbing openly as he scoops his son into a fierce hug.

"I'm going to guess you're my father," Zion says, a smile in his voice as Leo thumps his back in joy.

"Yes. I am so grateful to see you again, my son." Leo is beaming, clutching Zion like a trophy, the best gift he could ever receive.

When we enter the house, Gran Gran and Mackenzie are waiting just inside the doorway. Mackenzie is floating, her body wiggling with glee, and Gran Gran's face is split between shock, pride, excitement, confusion, and love. One after another, they wrap their arms around us—hugs and kisses and squeezes. Gran Gran makes a point to congratulate each of us—Lilo, Liberty, Aurora, and me.

"Me talk wit Kiara earlier, lawd, a lik a fi mi grandson, mi daughter, it fi you a dis sight me see, child. Me never tank ye enough, eh? Me 'quiet storm,'" she said, thumping my back with her arm.

Mom and Gran Gran share a long a tearful embrace. They must have missed each other terribly during their decades of silence.

Mackenzie falls in love with Zion immediately. "Hello! You are tall. Your arms are really, really big. Can you carry me on your back?" Minutes later he is giving her a piggy-back ride while she gives him a tour of the house.

My stomach grumbles loudly in response to the delicious aromas wafting from the kitchen. Finally we gather at the dining room table, and the nine of us gorge on oxtail, rice and peas, jerk chicken, roasted breadfruit, dumplings, and yam. We take turns telling our stories, connecting the puzzle pieces from the past few days, until we have made one big picture, clear and complete.

When they find out that Fanny handed Rora off to Vincent, the cousins exchange a look. They quickly excuse themselves from the table, muttering back and forth how much they hate Fanny. I smile, knowing they're up to some revenge scheme I will love hearing about later.

Mom tells us how she was drugged and snatched from the flight, that her father laughed in her face as he locked her in the freezer for days, monitoring her as she slowly lost her powers in the cold.

"One thing doesn't make sense to me, though," Mother says, looking to Gran Gran. "How was Father able to hide Zion from your visions?"

Gran Gran's eyes shift a light gray as she reveals that her call-ins with the Fates and visions about the family had been hazy for over a century. "Me tink it stress or dat me ad displeased de Fates, so me say noting. I neva know

Ezekiel was a use de science an interfere with me powers."

Once I bound Zion's memories, Gran was able to regain a view of his present and future, but not his past. She assures us the evil grip on his mind was gone. But she's still not able to view where Grandfather and her son Taresh had disappeared.

When everyone at the table turns to me, awaiting my story, I look around at the faces of my family, knowing they want to hear about my tactics, strategizing, and bravery, how I learned Kiara's power to call Mom, how we fought the Brotherhood and I wiped their memories, how we saved Mom, Rora, and Lilo from evil Zion and turned him good. I haven't even told anyone the full story of running into Grandfather before the battle yet. My head aches with all the places it's been. I know I will tell them everything in the days before we return to Ohio, but for now I say the simple sentence pounding through in my heart: "I did whatever I had to do to get our family back together."

A WEEK LATER, when we pull into our driveway in Cincinnati, Devin is sitting on our front steps. All the way home—on the airplane, in the car ride—I've thought of him, conjuring his face, his voice, his hands. Now my heart races, as he strides toward the car. *A goddess's heart calls to her true love when she is ready*, Gran said. And so, he is here.

I throw the car door open before the tires have stopped rolling and call out, "You do know stalking is one of those illegal type behaviors, right?"

He laughs, and I see in his eyes that he's been thinking

about me, too, tortured by dreams of us together and in love. He picks me up and twirls me around, and I laugh into his neck, which smells just as amazing as I remembered. Gran said my heart summoned him. Now that I am in his arms again, I believe her. Devin is part of my happy ending.

"Hey now, none of that," Leo says, getting out of the car. "Aren't you the hooligan from the party? You're real brave showing up here again."

Devin puts me down gently and straightens his shirt. "Sir, I mean no disrespect with your daughter. I'm just here to say hello."

"He's not my father; he's my godfather," I whisper to Devin.

"Wait, who's disrespecting my sister?" Zion says, coming out of the van, puffing his chest needlessly.

"Sissy, way to reel him in with the long-distance lasso!" Aurora chuckles, following Zion.

"Arden, is this your boyfriend? Please introduce us!" Mom says, fluffing her hair as she closes the passenger door.

"Everyone, seriously, a girl is trying to have a private conversation. Thank you for the backup, but I got this." I wave everyone inside the house. "Yup, I'll see you in a minute. Goodbye." Once the front door is closed, I turn back to Devin, fearing he's annoyed by my nosy family, but instead I see that he's smiling. "What?" I ask, as he wraps his arms around my waist.

"It's clear from their suspicion of me that your family adores you."

"I'm sorry. They're so embarrassing," I mumble, biting my lip.

He sighs and strokes my cheek. "You're adorable. There's nothing to be sorry about. You're precious goods, and you're well loved. I want to earn the right to love you like they do."

I sigh and lean into his strong chest. His heart is beating as fast as mine. The moment feels so perfect, I'm almost afraid to believe in it. Am I living in a dream? *No, this is what it feels like when everything is in its right place.*

"But can I say one thing without sounding like a wuss?"

"Okay." I look up into his gray eyes.

"I did not know you had such a very big older brother." He frowns.

I laugh. "I didn't either. It's kinda a long story." I look to the house and the curtains shift quickly. I shake my head and look back to Devin. "I should get inside."

"Yes," he says, holding my hand. "I'll let you go. Sorry not sorry on the semi-stalking," he smiles shyly.

"It's okay," I say, grinning. "I'm glad your mission was a success." I squeeze his hand, and he squeezes mine back, then laces his fingers through mine. I close my eyes and sigh quietly.

"So, I know you have to go in, and you're probably jet-lagged, but could I call you tomorrow night to ask you out?" He caresses the skin on the back of my hand. In his eyes I see how excited he is to start living the future he sees in his dreams. Me, too.

"Yes," I say, but suddenly I'm overwhelmed with shyness. I look down at the ground. This gorgeous, sweet guy wants and has been waiting for and dreaming of awkward, introverted, bookworm me? What do I know about being in a relationship? He can't want just me, the way I am, right?

The answer comes loud and clear: *Why not? You are a goddess, Arden. You deserve a true and deep love because that's what you give to everyone, naturally.*

I breathe deeply, holding this truth. I'm at the end of a journey that's made me stronger, more ready than ever for whatever comes next. I can be fearless in the love I give others, and I can be fearless in the love I demand for myself, too.

"Arden?" Devin whispers.

I look up into his lovely eyes and am speechless.

"I'm really glad you're home." He leans in, and we are kissing. His lips are soft, questioning, and teasing against my mouth. It feels amazing, and my entire body is tingling, and as my lips open, I hear a voice cry from the porch.

"No babies on the front lawn, okay?"

We turn to see Aurora peeking out from the front window

"Rora!" I scream at her, as Devin laughs. She closes the window, and Devin buries his face in my hair, breathing deeply.

"So *that* was pretty embarrassing," I frown, and he chuckles.

"One of these days we won't have an audience," he says.

"I can wait."

I blush and look away.

"I promise I'm leaving now," he yells to the house, then looks back to me with a grin. "But before I do, happy belated birthday." He hands me a wrapped package.

I can feel that it's a book. I smile widely.

"It's nothing big," he says, "My cousin was stationed

in Japan and told me about this story. I thought you might like it."

I open the package and find a copy of *Mai the Psychic Girl, Volume 1.* "Thank you!" I beam at him. "This is so thoughtful, Devin. I love this book. I've been wanting to read it again." I kiss his lips softly, then lean in for a warm hug. *Eighteen looks pretty good on you, Arden, the Psychic Goddess Twin.*

"I'll speak to you soon," Devin says.

I hold onto his hand when he pulls away. I can't deny that he belongs in the life I'm starting, and it doesn't feel right that he's leaving. *Be fearless, Arden.*

"You should come meet everyone. Like, officially, not as the random guy in my bedroom or stalker mauling me on the lawn," I say.

"So, as your boyfriend?" he smiles.

I gulp. "Wow, you're pushy," I say, my heart threatening to explode.

"'Wow, you're a pushy boyfriend,' you mean?" he wiggles his eyebrow at me.

"I don't think I said that . . ." I reply, feigning confusion, biting my lip to keep from smiling.

"You know what? It's okay, I can wait on the title. Because I know I'm going to earn it."

"And aren't we confident!?" I laugh, walking away from Devin's heat.

"Yes, well . . ." he shrugs. "It's not that complicated. It feels right in my dreams, and it feels right in real life. Can I mention how I'm genuinely enjoying the weirdness of our love story thus far?"

I smile at him over my shoulder. "Well, if you enjoy weird, then you're definitely at the right house. We couldn't be normal if we tried." I have a lot to tell Devin, but I know he'll be able to take it.

"Who wants normal? Beautiful things happen when you let life be what it is," Devin says simply.

I stop and turn around, speechless. His words summarize exactly the feelings dancing in my head. The universe, or my goddess heart, definitely did good picking this man for me.

"What's wrong?" he asks, reaching out to link his fingers in mine.

"Nothing, it's just . . ." I laugh at the irony. "I'm not used to people reading my mind." I kiss Devin's hand and then open the door. We cross over the threshold, but freeze at the sound of Mom shouting, "Aurora, why did four sets of neighbors leave messages about a party?" Followed by a scream. "And who cracked my mermaid painting?"

"Oh, shit," Aurora says, appearing from the hallway, her shoulders hunched in guilt. "I'm already hella busted for the rager. Arden, can you please, please just tell her you did the mermaid in?" She walks away assuming I will say yes. Typical.

"Welcome to my life." I say to Devin, shaking my head.

"Thanks. I'm quite happy to be here," he responds.

I smile and really feel the joy from my head to my toes. Even though our evil grandfather is still out loose, my family is safe and together again. We're home, and I'm happy to be here, too.

# Epilogue

*T*eresh sits on a plush grey couch, silently watching Ezekiel pace against the white-and-black-tiled floor of their London hotel. It is hours past midnight; two nights since Zion's confrontation with the twins. Teresh has watched his father grow more agitated in the last forty-eight hours than he has ever seen in his long life. Ezekiel has refused to eat or sleep. He will only pace the length of their suite, muttering, shaking his head, and smacking the walls hour after hour.

Teresh is full of thoughts. Thoughts about the fact that he and Ezekiel had raced away from the fight like cowards. Thoughts that Zion never met up with them at their safe house and was clearly defeated. Thoughts that Ezekiel's century-long plan for revenge and global domination had fallen completely apart. But still, as the hours roll on from day to night, Teresh says nothing.

"We have failed!" Ezekiel yells, slamming his fists against the wall like a child exploding into a temper tantrum. Teresh sighs at the outburst, thankful they reserved the entire floor and have no neighbors to complain about the noise.

"Ghani's latest vision has revealed that Zion is back in her arms along with Selene and the twins—or will be very soon. The twins are alive, the power has not been transferred, we have failed. Zion has failed. I have failed. I have failed. I. Have. Failed!" Ezekiel beats his chest between the words, marching back and forth in a continuous loop.

From the couch Teresh clears his throat, and Ezekiel looks up, seeming to notice his son for the first time in a while.

"Teresh. Speak to me. I know there must be many thoughts running through your mind." Ezekiel walks toward the couch, his arms outstretched. His voice cracking. "I never considered this outcome! I never thought it was possible—that Zion would fail!"

Teresh bites his tongue, struggling to contain his explosive thoughts. *He* had considered this outcome, oh yes. Ezekiel would never hear of it, of course. Could not conceive of anything less than Zion's success, overtaking the white world, and toppling Ghani and The Fates.

But for the first time, Teresh now has the advantage over his father. He is now the one with a plan for action. Teresh exhales loud and deep, standing up tall from his place on the couch, overcome by a feeling of power—like a dragon breathing fire for the very first time.

"Father . . ." Teresh begins in a low voice, but Ezekiel has continued his pacing and muttering.

"Father—stop!" Teresh commands sharply, his voice booming in the air. Ezekiel freezes and turns to his son, his eyes wild with madness.

"What do you have to say, Teresh? There is nothing you

can say to fix this! Nothing can make the future what we wanted now that Zion is lost! Nothing!"

Ezekiel rips an abstract painting from the wall and screams as he throws it, frame and all, towards Teresh's head. But Teresh holds up his arms and easily blocks the art, tossing it aside. He takes small steps towards Ezekiel, his shoes crunching on shattered glass and tile, never losing eye contact with his father. For a moment, Teresh sees Ezekiel shiver and shrink backwards. *Father is afraid of me?* he considers wildly, realizing that Ezekiel is now at his most vulnerable and has nothing, no one but Teresh. *Or, Father is afraid to lose me?*

Either way, Teresh finally holds the power between them. A slow smile creeps on his face as he begins again, but more gently this time.

"Father, do you remember what your deepest desire was, so many years ago? The thing you wanted the most of all, that began all of this plotting against Ghani and The Fates?"

"Yes, of course I remember." Ezekiel huffs, turning away. "It is still my deepest desire! To have the power to truly lead my people, my black men, to the prosperity I know we deserve in this life." He sighs, dropping his frame heavily into the large black leather armchair by the door. To Teresh, Ezekiel looks suddenly so small and weary, crushed by the weight of the world on his shoulders. "Giving Ghani and our daughters these powers . . . a waste! It should have been me and you, my son! We should have the power to bring black justice to this white world. We were robbed from the start. But I thought, what if a grandson . . ."

Ezekiel trails off, his shoulders drooping as he slumps in the chair, defeated.

"You are right, Father. We were robbed." Teresh puffs up his chest. "And who got the spoils that were meant for us?"

"Ghani. Your sisters. Your nieces. All of the women," Ezekiel sneers.

"Then that's who we go after to get what belongs to us," Teresh says, his voice turning ice cold.

Ezekiel's head snaps back to his son in surprise. "What are you saying?"

"In that order. We start with Ghani. Where it all began. We'll end her life and move onto my sisters and nieces. We'll keep going until The Fates themselves intervene. We'll get the power we deserve over their dead bodies." Teresh grinds his foot into the tile, crushing the glass to a fine dust. Without feeling, he imagines strangling the women of his family, draining the life from their bodies. *And Zion. I'll finally have the chance to kill him, too.*

Ezekiel stares at Teresh with wide eyes, rising from the chair as if suddenly revived. "My son," he whispers and folds Teresh into his arms.

They stand together, locked in silence for a long time. It is the first time Teresh can ever remember being held by his father. Part of him wants to brush off the embrace, to maintain a sense of power and distance from Ezekiel. But the other part, the larger part, never wants Ezekiel to let go. This was what he had always wanted. To be seen and adored and needed by his father. As he breathed in the scent of cigars and cinnamon and squeezed his father a bit tighter, Teresh knew he would do anything, kill anyone, to keep this feeling alive.

Eventually, Ezekiel pulls back, but he stares at Teresh, his eyes dancing with excitement for what is to come.

"Teresh, my son. I am ready."

# THE END

# ACKNOWLEDGMENTS

I feel completely blessed to have had many people come into my life and help guide my path toward this great accomplishment, my first published book. While it feels "on brand" for me to want to thank from the bottom of my heart every single person I've ever met, including and especially those who never thought I could do this, I want to focus these pages on the very stand-out figures that helped in the tremendous growth I experienced in the past five years as I became the author of this book.

My mom: The absolute fiercest mother goddess of them all. Everything she does for me comes from the deepest well of unconditional love. And even when she doesn't understand me or my ways, she has more belief in my spirit than could fill the galaxy. She is the true muse for this novel. She is the reason I faced my writing talents head-on (I said, okay, if I'm really writing a novel, this thing better get published, I have to do it for Mom). She is also the source of inspiration for the plot. So much of this novel is inspired by my mother and by our beautifully intense relationship, which is every color of the rainbow and their opposite tones all in one.

The other day, I recalled how when I was little, I honestly thought my mother could read my mind because she could always tell when I was trying to lie. Now, to have written a book about a mind-reading girl who gets it from her mama . . . I can't help but feel an overflow of gratitude to the source. Her love for me has made me who I am, in every way possible, and her very present existence in my life has made this novel a thing. There's too much to say for these pages, but it boils down to this: I love making art because it makes my mother proud that I am her daughter. Thank you so very much, Lady. I love you.

My big sis, Tracy: Jesus, this woman, my beautiful big sister . . . Look, I would be obsessed with her even if I wasn't her little sister, but then I am, so, yeah, I could go on for a decade about my beyond-love for her. The existence of this novel is greatly due to the earth-shaking example she has set in how to be a loving and courageous black young woman. She has empowered me when I've been weak, forgiven me when I've been horrible, and helped ignite my life force when I've thought I might not survive. She was also the biggest backbone in me making the leap to leave my career in fashion and focus on writing. I remember asking her if I should quit a job I hated to write the novel of my dreams, terrified that she would insist I do the "reasonable" thing, and her saying, like it was no brainer, "Yeah, do it. I got you." And she has had me, every single step of the way. There is no way I would be a writer with a book, much less a sane human, right now, without my most beloved Tracyann. Everybody deserves someone like her in their life. I am so very grateful she is in mine. Thank you for everything and more.

My eldest sister, Marsha: The long distance love of my life . . . when I was little and she in college, she was a beacon of hope and love to me. She would mail me books and special things from her voyages and encouraged me to think about traveling and adventuring through life, too. She begged me to write her letters. She said she loved and cherished my way with words, even though I felt my life was barely worth memorializing. I have spent most of my life pining for her company and trying to do something so I'll have a great story for her the next time we meet. I have thought about her constantly throughout this writing process, and I hope she loves this story. I also greedily hope she gives me hours of recap of every single thing she felt while reading it. Marsha, you are in these pages, and you are a deep part of why I believed this was possible. Thank you and I miss you.

Valerie, my other mother: I always love the part of the hero's journey when they meet their mentor . . . I still remember the rainy evening in 2014 when I attended Valerie's writing workshop for the first time. I had no idea for a novel or belief in myself as a serious writer, but I connected with her in a way I never have with any other writing teacher. Maybe it's because my soul is so at peace around her that without trying I'm able to blossom; maybe it's because when she speaks I feel transported through dimensions and time; maybe it's because I want to be like her and make her proud. Whatever the reason, the magic she wields as a writer, teacher, editor, and coach has had a powerful effect on me. Valerie helped me become a serious writer. Valerie helped make this book possible, from start to end. Valerie is incredible. Thank you for everything you are to me and the entire universe. (The twins each give their thanks, too.)

Ms. Smith: When a prophecy is fulfilled, homage is due to the Oracle who first spoke the word. She was my fourth grade English teacher, and she loved my writing in a way that was laser focused and prophetic. She was my personal Professor Trelawney; she was insistent that I was a naturally gifted writer, that I was born to create with words, and that I would write a novel one day. I, for my part, was confused why this lady was so impressed with the drivel I produced and had concerns about her sanity. While I was busy trying to disappear from the daily bullying afforded to a "black nerd," Ms. Smith submitted a poem I wrote to an anthology because she believed my writing was too good to not share. When it won an award and got printed in an all-youth publication, I still told her, "I'm not that good. It's just a little poem, it's not like I wrote a whole novel." And she said, "Oh, but you will." With such confidence that I went home and cried at the wonder of your deepest dream thriving outside of your own body and in someone not even related to you. Thank you, Ms. Smith. You were so right, all along.

My aunt Sheila: I remember what she said to me through my deepest depression, when the world felt bleak: "Write it out, baby." These words have become my saving grace. Through the darkness and into the light, I have felt her love and faith that I can do anything I want in this life. She helped make me believe I could be a writer. "There's always been artists in our family," she said, like I was meant to be exactly this. Thank you, Auntie. I am deeply grateful.

Erica: She and I got that "play cousin" thing down pat. We've known each other since we were four years old, wearing tutus in ballet. It's beautifully mind-boggling that Erica and I still enjoy each other's company so deeply after so many years and evolutions. I am ignited by her spirit and have been since forever. She is effortlessly fun-loving, bold, charismatic, giving, and adventurous. They could strand Erica on a deserted island somewhere and somehow she'd end up making it the party of the year. She used to inspire me to do stupid stuff like sneak around the YMCA with her after swim class, and seriously, she's made me a braver person just by allowing me to be next to her fire. If I am more naturally Arden, she is my Aurora. Thank you, "play cousin," for being in my life and helping inspire this story.

Channelle and Cleo: The inspiration for Liberty is my gorgeous London cousin Channelle, who has stayed with me, in spirit and mind, since we turned the city wild together in 2006. Along with her sister, my other cousin and the real life Leolidessa, Cleo, we adventured and talked and danced and made friends and rode every train and bus around London for five weeks. They taught me how to haggle and flirt and speak up when I was upset. We spent time with their godmother, a queen who insisted on calling me "Yankee" and who inspired a lot of Gran Gran's presence. I surrendered to a crazy, vagabond summer with family I felt I'd known forever but had actually just met, and it was everything I needed to start coming out of the emotional shell I had made for myself. I took so many notes and pictures of us, till the girls nicknamed me "Paparazzi," because I was deeply infatuated with how powerful and amazing I could feel around them. It still remains one of the best experiences of my life. This book is in a lot of ways a fantasy snapshot of that month. Thank you, cousins. *On February 9th, 2020, my beloved cousin Channelle was lost to us under sudden and tragic circumstances. Through my disbelief, pain, and overwhelming grief, I have felt our love story pulsing evergreen in my heart. Channelle always saw me as more fabulous than I could fathom. She adored my klutziness, my nerdiness, and my big open heart: the things I tried to hide the most. She, too, prophesized me writing a book way before I planned to myself. *How blessed am I to have had a best friend, cousin, and soul sister all in one?* I miss her so very much and feel I must live fiercer and braver because that's what she would want of me. I'm grateful this book immortalizes her as she was to me, a goddess on earth. I love you, Channelle, my Liberty, always and forever.*

Cara: This goddess was one of the first of my close friends to have babies, and woah . . . to watch her become a mother, to hear of her doing everything to make their existence as blessed as possible, and to see the woman she continues to evolve into has been a huge testament of love to me. Thank you, Cara, for sharing your truths and your titanium spirit. You are reflected in several of the characters of this novel and remain a beautiful inspiration in my life.

My father: My love of science fiction and fantasy storytelling is a direct result of the passion my father has for the genre. I can't imagine becoming the writer of this story had it not been for my childhood obsessions with *Dune, The Dark Crystal, Star Wars, Matilda, The Neverending Story, The Princess Bride, Labyrinth,* and *Charlie and the Chocolate Factory,* and every single one of those books and/or films was introduced to me, with deep reverence, by my father. His favorite pastime is watching a film and later dictating what would have made the story better. It's adorable and fun to witness his fervor. In another universe, my father is the most influential movie critic of all time. I am a proud "black nerd" whose father is a proud "black nerd." This book, for sure, is a "black nerd production." Dad, thank you. I hope you like it, though I'm quite sure you'll have notes. (Also, thanks for all the postcards).

Tulloch, my godfather: Have you ever been grateful beyond reason that someone is as kind to you as they are, especially when you feel like you have less than nothing to offer in return? Tulloch is a family friend who truly became my godfather through caring for me through the sickness and mental health struggles and unemployment that befell me after graduate school. I can still remember how, when I would tell a story about my day job hunting in NYC in 2010 (spoiler alert: there's a recession and no one is hiring), Tulloch would laugh and laugh till he was crying and clutching his stomach. It was the highlight of my day, getting to talk to him and spin my life into a story that would make him laugh, even when it made me want to cry. He would shake his head at my self-doubt, as if to say, "But you, girl are going to make it. I know this, you'll see." His belief in me is unshakable, even though he's seen me at my worst. He is the direct inspiration for the character Leo, and I am completely grateful for his influence in my life. Thank you, Tulloch, for being so very wonderful to me.

Drew: I can still vividly remember seeing *The Matrix: Reloaded* with you and the Meshuggeneh Ninja Clan in high school, and then gifting you my leather "Trinity" coat because I knew, deeply, that you had a love of cosplay like I did. Over the years you have given me support, laughter, art, jewelry, music, paints, advice, love, loyalty, and Burning Man. You inspire me to be a creator and a passionate, open-hearted human, and I've definitely made out like a bandit in this exchange. Your friendship is one of the most valuable treasures in my life. In another universe, we are very definitely a brother and sister creative wonder duo. Thank you so much, Oz. I can't wait to share this accomplishment with you.

Wild Women Book Club, Burning Man Tribe, Bay Area Writing Community: I have evolved rapidly as an artist because I have had the chance to be witnessed, and to witness others, in community. I remember reading my work at my very first open mic at The Octopus, and being stunned by how attentive the audience was, how easily people asked, "Where can I find more of your writing?" with complete confidence that I was prolific and published. I have been challenged and inspired and supported by these tribes. Thank you for showing up to my performances and asking how my novel is coming and giving feedback and listening to me complain about plot holes or editing or rejection letters. And to specific souls within these tribes, who know who you are, you have been my lifeline during my evolution into an author. Thank you for not only tapping into my art and productivity but also encouraging my heart and spirit. I hope you all enjoy this addition to our creative cauldron.

Patrons: To my supportive Patrons who have followed this journey on Patreon, I am so grateful for you. I have enjoyed updating you on this roller coaster and having you be an online container for the highs and lows. Thank you for knowing I have the continued belief in others to be a creator. Thank you.

My teams at She Writes Press and SparkPress: I feel so very lucky to have found publishers who deeply believe in my writing. Lauren Wise and Taylor Brightwell, you and your teams have been a dream to work with. Thank you for your clarity, talents, time, encouragement, patience, energy, and everything you have done to make this publication a reality. Additionally, every single one of the goddesses says, "Thank you."

## About the Author

photo credit: Rich Jarvis

YODASSA WILLIAMS is a powerful conjurer of black girl magic (70 percent Jedi, 30 percent Sith). A Jamaican American writer, speaker, and award-winning performing storyteller, alumna of the VONA/Voices Travel Writing program, and the creator of the podcast *The Black Girl Magic Files*, Yodassa (Yoda) launched Writers Emerging, a wilderness writing retreat for women of color and non-binary people of color, in 2019. She grew up in Cincinnati, Ohio, and currently resides in the Bay Area. *The Goddess Twins* is her debut novel.

# SELECTED TITLES FROM SPARKPRESS

SparkPress is an independent boutique publisher delivering high-quality, entertaining, and engaging content that enhances readers' lives, with a special focus on female-driven work.
www.gosparkpress.com

*Above the Star: The 8th Island Trilogy, Book 1,* Alexis Chute. $16.95, 978-1-943006-56-4. *Above the Star* is an epic fantasy adventure experienced through the eyes of three unlikely heroes transported to a new world: senior citizen Archie; his daughter-in-law, Tessa; and his fourteen-year-old granddaughter, Ella. In this other-worldly realm, all interests are at war, all love is unrequited, and everyone is left to unravel the truth of who they really are.

*But Not Forever: A Novel,* Jan Von Schleh. $16.95, 978-1-943006-58-8. When identical fifteen-year-old girls are mysteriously switched in time, they discover the love that's been missing in their lives. Torn, both want to go home, but neither wants to give up what they now have.

*Tree Dreams: A Novel,* Kristin Kaye. $16.95, 978-1-943006-46-5. In the often-violent battle between loggers and environmentalists that plagues seventeen-year-old Jade's hometown in Northern California, she must decide whose side she's on—but choosing sides only makes matters worse.

*The Alienation of Courtney Hoffman: A Novel,* Brady Stefani. $17, 978-1-940716-34-3. When 15-year-old Courtney Hoffman starts getting visits from aliens at night, she's sure she's going crazy—but when she meets a mysterious older girl who has alien stories of her own, she embarks on a journey that takes her into her own family's deepest, darkest secrets

# About SparkPress

SparkPress is an independent, hybrid imprint focused on merging the best of the traditional publishing model with new and innovative strategies. We deliver high-quality, entertaining, and engaging content that enhances readers' lives. We are proud to bring to market a list of *New York Times* best-selling, award-winning, and debut authors who represent a wide array of genres, as well as our established, industry-wide reputation for creative, results-driven success in working with authors. SparkPress, a BookSparks imprint, is a division of SparkPoint Studio LLC.

Learn more at GoSparkPress.com